Ira,

Lickable Wallpaper

by
James Gabriel

Please accept this
As A Bit of my own exposure

James Gabriel
22527 Mountain Laurel Way
Diamond Bar, CA

ISBN-10: 1-934478-15-6
ISBN-13: 978-1-934478-15-8

FOREWORD

So how did all of this come about? This is my fourth novel, even though it's only my second to be published… self published that is. With four novels under my belt and quite literally no publishers or agents really willing to even look at my work I asked myself one question: If I could successfully publish just one novel and never make it with any other, which one would I want my name on and to be known for? The answer to that question was Lickable Wallpaper. It is my most important work, beyond anything I have written thus far and it is a piece of my soul. I would like to give it to the world. The idea of self-publishing struck me as something different from the last time, because honestly online publications eat your revenue. If you have a name and can promote, then putting something online might get you a bit of return, if not, you will only see pennies from it. I decided how many books I wanted and how much it would be to get it published through a publisher. After getting everything set up, I would presell 150 copies of the book and allow that to pay for the publication. Two weeks after coming up with the idea, my cousin Michelle discovered and sent me the link to a fundraising website. Fundable.com allowed me to set up and begin the process. There is a catch however. You only have twenty five days to raise the money. So I went on a begging frenzy asking everyone I knew for ten dollars. This was a monumental undertaking, but well worth it for I learned who would support and who would snub. Some "friends" went so far as deleting and blocking me from their lists after a few emails. It got a good start, then slowed down severely and if it wasn't for some very amazing friends that donated much more than their share, I honestly would never have succeeded and you would not be reading this right now.

So I would like to give special thanks and acknowledge those for their contributions that led to this great possibility for me. Jennifer Upstill, Chris Hebert, Del Leon, Isabel Zamarripa, Harry Grammer, Ariana Hall, America Solis-Bowman, Koji S Sakai, Michele De Rouen, Greg Bellows, Genevieve De Rouen, Suzanne

Bressler, Thomas Lewis, Ingo Janetschek, Gina Cortez, Fred Benavidez, Tina Wright, Danielle De Rouen, Robert Giles, Nicki Somerville, Rodney Gray, Maria De Rouen, Holly Novell, Malinda De Rouen, Micah Miller, Tyrone Easter, Joseph McGovern, David De Rouen, Lisa Dinkins, Ernie Silva, Stefanie Brant, Teresa Metoyer, Cynthia Bolander, Sheava Rahimi, Darice Clark, William Martin, Michelle Craine, Carter Dewberry, Marisa Foegen, Heather Aymie, Rick Lupert, Travis Cutler, Sean Hurdle, Sylton Hurdle, John Schumacher, Linda Medina, Sabrina Jones, La Toya De Rouen, Richard Procello, Giovanni Fascio Jr., Danno Metoyer, Diana Aguiar, Lisa Metoyer, Anne Fascio Ramirez, Henry A. & Muriel A. Leon, Dominique De Rouen. From the bottom of my heart you are all truly a part of making this book happen, all my love and thanks to you all.

James Gabriel
October 13, 2007

An Assimilated Agent

...IT WAS HIS FEET that drew me at the first sight and though the how's and why's might cause some undue embarrassment, I must in fairness, explain how I came to be stalking this person, miles through the streets of the city over the last hour. It was a good evening and that's saying something because my frustration of late has had me twisted with constipated energy continually asking myself "What now?"

The difficulty in creating not withstanding, the want of finding a place for my completed works is a hulking bitch looming over my every thought. I am not one of those thinking death is stalking me, at least not yet. No, for me it is this destined thought that life cannot begin or continue until I succeed. And succeed is a broad term meaning I am doing what I want with my life, whatever that is, being self-sufficient of course. I have to work, but I want to be working for myself. These are the thoughts that run through my head as I follow the enormous mound of walking individual thirty yards up the sidewalk in front of me, as I navigate the crowd of people. I must explain though, all of this began in the contemplative compromising position of a restroom toilet.

I had awaited the opportunity to purge much longer than I deemed necessary, outside the stalls with my stomach in agitated disagreement over some unfortunate seafood. My luck was to have the rumbling urge squelch me suddenly in a large chain bookstore in the midst of a concert by a mostly unknown local singer.

There once was a boy who lived with his mother, in a house, near some woods… That looked like the beginning of something, but so what? I thought, closing my Moleskin with regret. The truth of frustration is when you're not blocked, because I can write other things, poems, work on a short story or something, but lately I have been under the distinct impression that something has been trying come through. I think that, could be the beginning of a children's story and I don't write children's stories for the most part. They tend to get twisted in the telling. Then again there was something about it that felt different, off, foreign, as if it was coming from some other place, elusive and strange. I looked at the words. With such a simplistic beginning I began to imagine this little boy bent into some dark place of magic, but that wasn't going to fit either.

Lately I find myself existing in a state of perpetual déjà vu, as if all reality had the good sense to step around me in avoidance. I moved, a singular cartoon entity in a flesh world. Still, there was a child borne in me, and my only question to myself was, where was all this headed? I manipulated the line. *I once saw a child, a little boy living…*

A college professor once told me there is a small percentage of the world that sees reality as a cartoon, as if the world we live in is false, and the world of colored drawings on television is reality. At least they see it as reality. When he asked me what I thought about that I replied, "Who says it can't be?"

"Exactly," he exclaimed, patting me on the shoulder and walking on.

I think the comment was in response to the enthusiasm and creativity I displayed in his class, but I don't know. Another professor once asked me out of the blue if I had traveled much. I hadn't and when I told him so he said that I gave the distinct impression of someone who had traveled a great deal. I don't know what that meant either. These, I'll have you know, both took place years before I even thought about writing. During this time I was an art major and not working nearly as hard as I write now.

Bookstores had become my refuge of late and I entered, moving to the section to find my own among the volumes in my mind, rows of words stolen-bound. I read like a fiend. I passed the metaphysical section, many of which I had on my shelf at home, some of which I knew verbatim. I hadn't read any of the new ones in awhile as I have found many were beginning to sound rehashed and trite, overdone.

I love imagery in stories that bring pictures to mind like movies. I love movies. I find it illuminating that individuals passed on from these moments have continued to live. Their essence has graced that bit of celluloid-digital immortality and I wonder if some bits of them remain. If beloved they could very well span the race of mankind. In books, authors adopt images of individuals in phrase-photography, the imagined creation of things, which may or may not exist, though afterwards, the essence of it certainly must. Thought is the basis of reality and on the page they are bound into minds, beyond the pages, into all those who read them.

Imagine ghosts, confined-incomplete, to a place. Holding never the desire to be a figure in silhouette, spoken about from a detached voice, etched into a page of verse. Written with or without love or adoration by those who told storied emotions. Entities, strewn of ink-black phantoms running together over dead-leafed parchment, never wanting to be sentenced to life extended with a possibility of immortality, long after desires have flickered and life has passed. Shelves of rowed text, modern and old, filled with others who never asked among new creations spawned from old. A life borne, breathed by pen and type. Stories of private moments, real or imagined unveiled for the world to judge levels of discretion and decency from the now past. Held and cherished until death parts or a match struck breaches four hundred fifty-one degrees of misery, violated by time. Then, once again, back to shelves to gather dust, lost, remembered to be forgotten, over and again…and again.

In the bookstore my stomach rolled with the meal I had consumed earlier in the evening and I decided I needed to use the restroom before I got a cup o' coffee or found a spot to settle into. There was a thick crowd and the upstairs had an audience watching a woman playing on a shiny, obsidian baby grand. She had a good voice and the piano was hot, so I held for a moment to take in the show. She, dressed in black with a 'Super S' stenciled in gold on her t-shirt, said she was from Vegas and I pictured this girl as a lounge singer and wondered if Billy once started like this henna-blond piano woman, thick with age, though she proclaimed possibly stunning, dropping hints of her enjoying a tickle on the 'F' key.

Around the bookstore the wanderers of note, are not of the same audience found in a Vegas lounge. In this place I'm sure the microphone smells like old coffee, which saturates the surrounding shelves echoing the tragedies spun into her lyrics. Her persona has me finding her much more comfortable in a Broadway rock opera than in this chain bookstore with ogling stares churning in the caffeinated air of bebop. She spoke of her father as she played a song called "The Preacher" on a Baby Grand, echoing big glossy-black healing tones with teeth stained ivory and obsidian. In my current frustration I found myself wishing I knew her before she was here. Before she was super, changed and saved lives with her music. Before she grew up. When she was just a girl.

I left in the applause and adjourned to the restroom where I found a short line and waited. The necessity of urinals in the men's restroom not withstanding, there is a sense of uneasiness when the urinals are vacant and there is a line waiting for the stalls, especially when you are in that line. There will be, unfortunately, no escape for you or them to the effect a hefty male sit-down could have on the space.

A friend of mine had a joke for that waiting moment. He would curl his index finger to his thumb like the sign for 'okay', and hold it to his face with his nose sticking through the hole. "It's like this, it's like this." He would announce to anyone around, showing the tip of his nose as he waited for the moment it was time to adjourn to the toilet and "drop the kids off in the pool."

His sense of humor had several lines in that particular vein.

He stepped out of the bathroom looking distraught one day and told me, almost in a whisper, "Man I can't believe those two are still together after all that shit."

Store gossip always being a grand topic I curiously asked, "Who?"

"My ass cheeks," he said and began to laugh.

I have come to understand that the twisting of the waist is one way the body helps in digestion. When the waist turns the innards move and it affects the intestines and thereby affects the colon as well.

One day while sitting in break room he stepped in announcing, "It's like this." his nose pushing through the okay sign.

"Hey." I said. "Stand with your feet planted and bring your arms around to twist your waist as far as you can."

He looked at me strangely for a moment, planted his feat and turned.

Without another word he ran straight into the bathroom.

Thinker

THE FIRST GLIMPSE I received of the man I am following was through the stall break as I stood waiting for my turn. He moved about in the largest which is supposed to be reserved for the handicapped, though rarely have I seen them used for that section of the population. I must admit if I have a choice I much prefer doing my business in the handicapped stalls because they are so big, much bigger than the little area where the toilet resides in my bathroom The jacket, rather than bumping into the sometimes-untouchable walls in the smaller ones and have a real sit down if necessary.

The people before me in line stepped into the other two stalls as their occupants flushed and stepped out. I waited for the next one to become available which should have been the big one giving the timing of an average individuals business. I was hopeful, but even as I observed movement beyond the door he did not emerge. This effectually caused me even more frustration as I mistakenly anticipated my personal relief coming soon. At one point I glimpsed the top of his salt and pepper head and I anticipated his height somewhere over six feet, determined by my the angle of my view against the height of the stall.

I had not seen his feet at this point and *at this point* I wish to discourage any sort of fetishism on my part though I did observe that the shoes in the other two stalls sat patiently handling their business.

There was a Saturday Night Live skit that took place in a men's restroom. Most of the skit only showed the feet sitting in the stalls that suddenly broke out into an a capella rendition of "Under the Boardwalk" The shoes in all the stalls tapped in time to the chorus except one, the lead singer whose loafers danced and bopped to lyrics backed up by the other shoes... It was funny and I smiled now thinking about it realizing how nonsense it was, of course comedy doesn't have to make sense, in fact it's sometimes better if it doesn't.

I waited.

The shoes in the middle stall moved, shuffled a bit, flushed, then stepped out and I entered, prepared and sat, thinking about nothing in particular other than my current matter of business and reading the words scratched on the walls. It wasn't graffiti, that stuff is colored and beautiful. Most of it wasn't tagging either because that is usually written in an almost indecipherable scrawl similar to the Wingdings font. This stuff was at least readable.

"Fuck the war" someone had written, and there was a response written by someone else. *"Fuck you I was in the war, World War II, sometimes it's necessary."*

I find that bathroom walls are directly connected with the environment and intelligence level of the demographic in that environment. Bookstores could have a higher literacy record compared to other places like hardware stores, gas stations or malls, with racial epitaphs, gang signs and affiliations.

"In life we dread the thought of death. Perhaps it is that in death we dread the thought of life," was written in red on the other wall. Yes, environment and education obviously had something to do with the intelligence level of tagging.

"He is the way and the light, only through him will you be saved."

Response: "If you see him could you have him give me a call."

Another: *"This search is yours."*

And finally: *"Hey I think I found him, look down."*

I heard movement in the handicapped stall followed by a deep grunt and then the foot stepped into view.

The foot.

The biggest I have ever seen or imagined was held by a few famous basketball players' whose shoe sizes are on display in a many native sports shrines which I have had the misfortune of wasting hours of my time in. This one dwarfed all of them. It was wrapped in a large black sandal, but the appendage was so wide it spilled around the edges and the base had been squeezed into a puffy cushion of skin framing it with stretch marks as if it were threatening to burst. The owner of that must be extremely heavy I surmised and if this had been the only curiosity I would have returned to my business without a thought, but the toes of this hoof were the most interesting of all.

The big toe of the mammoth pad was like a sausage. It started early and reached out beyond the others and past the tip of the sandal to curl beneath the next toe and a portion of the other. By my word if that failed to strike me on some way, the other toes did it. Each was quite long and knurled with thick nails that came out and curled down, almost as one would imagine a claw. Ideally it had no business displaying itself in a sandal of any type, but it thoroughly escaped me as to what shoe would enclose such a foot. I was suddenly struck by the image that it did not belong to a man, but some sort of troglodytian creature like the Moorlocks from Wells' Time Machine and it was then that I decided I needed to see what this person looked like, if not learn who he was altogether.

As a result I doubled my efforts to finish my business which was no small task and my straining had me afraid of causing an aneurysm. The foot stepped out of the stall and I heard the sink turn on for a short moment, then off. I quickly wiped and buckled my pants, with a sudden air of thanks when I heard the drone of the hand dryer.

I stepped out.

Mongo

THE MAN (if I could say that and not offend him) was easily two, perhaps three of me wide. He stood gently rubbing his hands beneath the dryer in a textbook fashion, though what air could make it around those manacles I could not tell. The hands were the size of baseball mitts and one could have easily swallowed my entire head. There was no way I could reach the sink as he blocked most of the counter, so I waited, giving him a good once-over. The hair on the back of my neck rose when I looked up into his face. Six foot three, with a head like a barn door, calmly rubbing his hands together as he glanced down around his shoulder at me through narrow slits. I froze in that moment before the dryer shut off and he moved.

I jumped, realizing I had been staring. He took a hunched shuffled step towards the door and it escaped me how he was going to get through, not only that, but how the hell had he gotten in here in the first place. It didn't occur to me then and would be almost a half hour later when I noticed the strange squatted position he walked in had him hunched and if he stood fully upright, his standing height would have him towering somewhere very beyond eight feet. I splashed some water on my hands and chased out the door after him.

In the store, I watched as the big man slowly meandered through the crowd of isles and people. Oddly, no one took any notice of him at all. Now, I am not one to stare at the malformed, dwarfed, retarded or in this case gigantic, but this person is unlike anyone I have ever seen in my entire life and I'm quite certain no one in the store had ever seen anyone like him either. Therefore, a glimpse, or some sort of double take would be warranted in this case, but it wasn't to be, he simply made his way down the isles to the front door and exited without notice.

I am not sure why exactly I decided to follow him at this point. Curiosity was certainly a factor and such an easy term to use, but it was something else that overcame me. A silent driven hunger I could not explain. I had to follow, if only to continue to observe and perhaps learn more about this being that my current perceptions had stepping from the pages of horror classics, strange tales and circus legend. He wasn't homeless, of that I was positive. His clothes though extremely large were clean and had no foul scent of the city's undertow. Other than the hunched stature of this gargantuan "Mr. Hyde" he could have been any persons grandfather with a bad back and a touch of scoliosis.

On the street I was shocked again to see the same reaction by everyone he passed as in the bookstore. It was as if the world had been raised in Barnum's circus and witnessed individuals like this everyday.

He turned onto another street and it was now that I began to question my own sanity.

Sanity is based on perception and only determined by a given point of view. Everyday, people make thousands of decisions that keep themselves sane. The urge to say, "fuck it all" and hop on a plane, away from life, check out, or simply loose it in a person that irritates you, attacking and smashing that little grin they have until they will grin no more. Sexual fantasies and urges normal and strange. Road rage would truly be, if you smashed your car into some stupid asshole that desperately deserved it. People sitting on benches talking to lampposts and buildings do not question their reality. The neighbors that believe you're a prick for some obscure reason are also living in world of their own point of view. Perhaps the aneurysm brought this on and I snapped. Perhaps I'm passed out in the toilet right now imagining all of this while waiting for my body to be discovered. Or maybe people like this have existed my entire life and for some obscure reason I never noticed them before.

I was beginning to dread the obvious, that the man didn't exist at all and I was just chasing a figment of my imagination, when it happened. He bumped into someone. The man he bumped into stumbled back. Who wouldn't, colliding with four to five hundred pounds of wall encased in flesh? There was simply no expression on the man's face when he turned to look up at who it was that had bumped into him. He said something I couldn't hear, probably "excuse me" and walked on. By the time I passed by him, the man was stone faced and unaware. This left me with the knowledge that I was not following my imagination and to finalize my belief, I took a pinch of skin on my arm and squeezed and twisted until I felt the pain was sufficient that I knew it wasn't imagined.

This must be real.

A half block was the only distance I allowed between us, any closer and he might notice, turn and confront me, which honestly terrified me, but if I allowed any greater distance I feared I would loose him.

The streets were crowded at first, but the farther we went the more it thinned and the area became less and less familiar to me. The buildings were becoming more decrepit and rundown, even the people began to... look? no, feel different is a better description, though I was uncertain exactly what the difference was. The streets weren't crowded, but the shadows began to feel ominous. Every person I passed had me uneasy as if I was not welcome. Nothing around held any familiarity and I wondered how I was going to find my way back. With all the twists, I hoped I didn't need to get out of here fast for some reason, because now it was me getting stared at rather than the big man who one would assume is much more of an oddity.

He turned down another street and when I stepped around the corner I stopped. It was almost completely deserted and the atmosphere felt very wrong somehow. I began to follow and stopped again. He was almost halfway down the street, but if he turned around there would be no place to hide. The irrational obsession, which had possessed me for, I checked my watch, almost an hour was not going to be abandoned now. I walked a bit down the street then jutted across quickly advancing as I did so, so I could still keep him in sight. A small group of women dressed for the "evening" were milling on a stoop. They all saw me.

From their looks my first reaction was to run. My skin began to crawl with a consuming fear as if I was illegally trespassing in someone else's property, and was about to be reported. The women looked away pretending not to notice. All but one. I hadn't noticed her standing at the top of the stoop. She was almost completely hidden in shadow and the dim light seemed to help her blend with the building's column. She was extremely tall and anorexic thin. The light colored sheer cloth she wore, blended with her pasty skin and blond hair that camouflaged her against the wall of the building, but when she stepped out her eyes were focused directly on me.

I shrunk.

Her skin was death. Fragile and taunt like rubber stretched to its absolute limit. All the women looked like this, greasy/pale with too much make up and wrong body types slinking beneath lingerie. Mannequins of a horror show come to life. When she stepped out her eyes suddenly went wide with shock. She opened her mouth to speak, but said nothing and I decided to take my chances with the big man. I re-crossed the street, not wanting to actually pass by the women on the stoop. I looked back twice to see the women were still watching me, all eyes open in silent accusatory terror.

A Less-Traveled Verge

I FIND IT A STRANGE JUSTIFICATION that though I was secretly following this man, I felt safer going where he went rather than traversing the strange streets I had never been down before and make my own path. Not that he would protect me from what I had come to believe would be an almost certain level of demise. These people were not like regular people at all. If I paid any attention to the caveat voice in my head I would certainly believe that my sanity had gone on leave.

What was I thinking, I asked myself, and that's when I realized, I wasn't thinking right now. I was reacting on instinct, drive, the same instinct that had lead me an hour away from my car, outside of familiar areas and now had me walking in some part of the city that, at the moment, I would equate with some of the rougher more undesirable neighborhoods. Perhaps the big man knew this and I was being lured into some sort of ominous trap.

I was far too close now and watched as he turned again, this time into the pitch darkness of an alley and in my paranoia, I thought I saw him glance at me when he did so…

That slowed my step for a moment and I looked back again to the stoop to see if the tall lady was still staring at me. The stoop was now deserted and left only a dim porch light illuminating it. I was utterly alone and the street became suddenly very large. I approached the alley where the big man had gone and the darkness refused to recede when I looked down it. There was a light at the end and I believed I saw the big mans hunched movement, but I was uncertain. There was no turning back at this point. I glanced behind me again and realized how utterly alien the street looked to me. The streetlamps themselves did not shine, but only released some sort of half-assed glow into the air like it was gas. The houses that had porch lights as the stoop where the women had been standing, and even with this eeriness everything seemed to be alive with its own unnatural anima.

The street knew I was there and it was watching me, and as I stared down this block, it suddenly changed.

In the military when soldiers are trained to sneak up on someone they are told to watch their target's ankles, not to stare at their back or the back of their head because the target will sense someone staring at them and turn. Just as the blind can sense when there is another person in the room, I no longer sensed the street living. The street was alive. The trees, the plants and buildings themselves suddenly awoke. Nothing moved mind you, but in that moment I never stood in a more alien environment in my life. I looked down the pitch-black alley again and could now easily see the big man near the end where the only light shown, but that light too had begun to dull. I panicked. I glanced back at the street only a moment to see that many of the lights had now gone dim or been swallowed by the dark altogether, a few now only appeared as flickering candles. In the distance a breeze started like the moan of breath and I felt my hairs stand on end.

I ran.

The alley swallowed me as if filled with a thin black soup. Ever try to spank a dog that already knows it's in trouble and running away? It drops its tale and tucks its ass under itself in an effort to evade the last strike, sometimes they yelp even if there is no contact, sensing how very close it was. That was me now. I felt the dark saturating me, attempting to slow my pace and somehow I knew there was no longer any separation between alley and street, inanimate and life. The big man turned left in the light at the end and I wasn't even halfway through.

The moment he was out of sight I felt the walls began to collapse. I was in something's throat.

I tried to run faster and felt the wind again as breath or was it that I was running so fast, I couldn't tell. My only thought was catching up to the big man. I was almost at the end when my tail dropped for the second time. I believe I yelped because the wind had gotten warm and was now coming from behind me. I had the thought of diving, but instead, pushed harder to beat the light still fading in front of me. I shot out of the alley across the sidewalk and into the street to the left, looking for the big man, terrified of looking back to see what might suddenly come bursting out of the alley in pursuit.

From two doors down, people turned to stare at me. There

were four tables out in front of a little coffee shop that... I scanned the area to get my bearings, looking for the big man who was nowhere I could see. The street went on a few more doors, but he couldn't have gotten that far and besides, I was back... I recognized this area.

A horn blared and I jumped. A car had stopped behind me rather than run me over. I moved to the sidewalk with a sheepish grin avoiding the alley and a waved the car by. I knew this area, at least I thought I did. The name on the awning read Pantheons. I did know this place, but I couldn't have traveled this far in all this time. It had been an hour and I wasn't so completely twisted that I had missed traveling a few blocks in a circle.

Pantheon

PANTHEONS WAS LOCATED about eight blocks from the bookstore, a fifteen-minute walk if there was one. I tried to retrace my route, but there was no way we could have gotten here... because we went the opposite direction. I thought of the big man, the twists and turns of the journey and looked both directions up the street searching for him. The only place he could have gone was inside. Perhaps he was in the restroom again. One of the tables outside was unoccupied so I dropped my moleskin and entered the coffee shop to stares from people seated at the outside tables. I didn't come here often, but enough that it held a familiarity to me, and at the same time the place that was just a bit out of sorts and strange, very like the last hour I had spent walking. At least it was comfortable.

Inside I was ignored and I made my way to the restroom. There was only one and the door read occupied. I couldn't stand in front of it waiting. What would I do when he stepped out and saw me? I know he saw me in the restroom at the bookstore and I didn't want to have him think I was stalking him, which of course I was. I moved to the counter, past the fortune-telling woman sitting beside it and waited for the couple ahead of me to finish ordering. I was a little hungry and my stomach was no longer hurting. The walk must have done me some good.

It wasn't too late in the evening. The crowd really hadn't

shown up yet, but the regulars were there. The fortune-telling woman sat in her regular spot. The tall pale woman dressed in black behind the counter was the manager. I figured she had been a typical eighties Goth chick. Her black bangs half covered her eyes that had too much black eyeliner. In the corner, the older English looking guy sat reading as usual at a table by the front window on one side of the door. By the other window sat Twill in his usual spot reading the newspaper. I don't remember the last time I was in here, but the strange thing I must confess is that I have never heard his name nor been introduced to him, but from the first moment I saw him, in my head I called him Twill.

I ordered a large coffee and a cookie. I didn't know how long I would be following the big man for so I figured I should get something to keep me going. I paid the girl behind the counter whose badge read Noaisha. I smiled, she didn't. I stepped to the side for cream and sugar and I heard the boor behind me open, mentally picturing the big man emerging hunched, lumbering as wide as three people across the floor towards the front door as I hurriedly doctored my coffee… I turned and observed a guy stepping to the counter from the restroom. He gave the key back to Noaisha and then returned to a table with two half finished drinks and a girl.

I scanned the coffee shop in a panic. I had fucked up! I left my coffee and cookie and went to the restroom forgetting I needed a key and pulled the locked handle that didn't give.

"You need a key sir."

"Yeah." I said grabbing it. Shit, how long had it been? A block? Two maybe three ahead of me and I didn't know which direction. Shit! I opened the door anyway to the empty room and briefly thought about chasing after the big man before I came to my senses and relaxed. Shit!

I let door close and went back to my coffee dropping the key on the counter with a quick, "Thanks," to Noaisha. I doctored my coffee and took the cookie to sit at the last unoccupied table outside, disappointed. The most I could do now was write about the experience. I made sure my back wasn't to the alley and since I knew where I was, I was now glad I didn't need to retrace that route myself.

I got situated and noticed the other regular, Drover, also always here. Drover was homeless, with a face of black mocha hidden behind a beard beneath an Afro that never really grew too wild. Drover was a watcher of people always in blue sweats as cars casually passed the nomad, who I felt called life home. He sat on the flower box in front of the hair salon next door as I watched him look up the street and down again, always content.

The night was cool and I opened my moleskin and stared at the mostly blank page I was on. What the hell was I going to write? About how I saw this guy in a bathroom stall and decided to stalk him? I don't think so. I'd sound like a pervert, a weird pervert at that. I read the last page over again, two lines. *There once was a boy who lived with his mother, in a house, near some woods… There once was a child living…* I felt certain that it wanted to go somewhere.

I turned to a blank page, broke off a piece of cookie and took a sip of coffee.

Olympus

WHEN I FINISHED THE COOKIE I was still staring at blank pages. I thought off the big man again and glanced around the area, half expecting him to cross the street at the corner, but it didn't happen. I sat back, started to watch the people coming a going and the others sitting outside with me. It was a good night and I was happy to be outdoors, away from my job and the backroom cubicle with sour recycled air, and a bad coffee/pastry addiction beneath brain numbing fluorescents. Across from me I noticed the kid, a slightly mocking bit of irony as he sat reading the most popular book in the world while I struggled for plot ideas. In the window just behind him, Twill sat reading the weekly and I noticed regularly lowered his paper to stare at me through the glass for a moment then go back to his paper again.

I always liked the atmosphere of Pantheons and this part of town in general. This was the playhouse district and though Pantheons was semi-chic, the old brick of the building held more nostalgia than the establishment's attempt at society art life.

The Reading Kid pulled a tobacco tin from his shoulder bag, popped the top, found a pack of zigzags and began to roll a cigarette as Twill looked up at me again.

There were three other tables outside besides mine. The Reading Kid at one, an older couple sat at another observing the night in quiet conversation, having learned long ago how to keep one to themselves. At the last table a young guy and girl whom it was obvious regularly watched all the latest pop culture television drama, loudly discussed the legitimacy and legalities of downloading.

"Well honestly I don't think they will come after me," the guy at the other table said. "I mean what, five hundred songs?"

He was a little effeminate and wore all name brands, probably right down to his thong.

"They're going after everyone now." The girl, just too squeaky and complacent in her loud pretension, I thought needed to be slapped, and by the couples glance towards her, they agreed. Her tude-filled voice grated on nerves.

"Noooo." He shuffled the word towards the girl with far too much expression. "They're looking for the ones with thousands. Jeremy has something around like twelve thousand. They should go after him."

I got the feeling he'd gladly sell out this Jeremy if the authorities came after him. Actually I think they both needed to be slapped.

The uninterested opinions of their conversation arose in my head and shit all over my consciousness as I was sucked in.

Idea: to regulate downloading, take an average number of songs per album, average price (bargain) for each album and make the fine equal to the sum total of that, divided by how many "illegal" songs the person has. That way the government can levy the fines, and be sure to catch as many as possible big or small. All of the money should go to the owner of the songs, however the bushwhacked government probably won't proceed unless they are getting something out of it. So, a percentage (small) of the fines should go to the government and the rest to the owner of each song. Public domain is of course exempt.

"The government is getting involved now." The girl said. "And with the monitoring capabilities they have, I figure everyone is going to get caught eventually." The nothing tone of pretend knowledge drew on and every so often they would laugh so loudly people inside would look out. "You know they said they're going to restart the draft."

"No they aren't."

"Yeah huh."

"I don't care," he crossed his legs. "I wont go. Can you imagine me with a gun? Me?"

"I would," The girl said. "I can shoot a little."

I couldn't imagine this girl mending a fence. It pains me to say I have friends with this same mentality; fear based and ready to kill anyone that thinks or looks different, prays to a different God, or says we aren't allowed to spend our money on cars and cable.

"I don't see why we don't just go over there and kill them all." She finished.

"It isn't all of them doing it you know. There are innocent people."

"So what, they're killing us. We should just nuke them and be done with it. Even Adrian thinks so."

I wasn't sure if Adrian was a guy or a girl, but a face came to mind. Actually a face didn't, more of a mental picture of someone's brain, someone speaking, someone just as annoying and in need of a wake-up bitch-backhand-pimp-slap as these two.

The Reading Kid had already finished his cigarette and had his nose back in the book.

"Did you see the Grammy's?" the guy asked, changing the subject. I think he was uncomfortable with the girl talking so matter-of-factly about genocide, but didn't want to lose his "girlfriend".

"No,"

"Well you know last week, Britney?"

"Yeah."

"Same thing again, but who is she?" He stared waiting for her to agree.

"Yeah, I mean, so what. Who does she think she is? I saw her on six other shows last week."

"Me too she was everywhere, like what's up with that. Enough already." He seemed to be mostly upset that he wasn't her…

The two continued their talk, now both jealously bashing celebrities they were not like, didn't know and would never be. I turned back to the Reading Kid and looked past him to find that Twill was gone, the abandoned paper folded neatly on his stool, which was only strange by the fact that in my mind he never moved from that spot.

I turned to a small group of people approaching from somewhere down the street, out from one of the theaters or restaurants. They passed Drover, mostly ignoring him as mostly everyone did. Every so often though, people would pause and stare at him, intently transfixed by something imperceptible, strange. Sometimes words were exchanged, but not often. I once saw a girl breakdown into heavy tears, turn and run back to her car and drive away.

There were six in the crowd and one of the men stopped his girlfriend as they stepped pass the brick flower box with Drover seated on it and stared at him. The guy stood transfixed as Drover looked up at him. His girlfriend glanced back and forth between the two for a full minute calling her boyfriends name "David…David…" over and again. Finally the boyfriend's shoulders relaxed and he released a smile that beamed. He calmly reached into his pocket, pulled out some money and gave it to Drover, then took his girlfriends arm and led her to catch up with the friends who had already entered the coffee shop.

"What was all that?" she asked.

"What?" he asked as they went inside.

I turned back to Drover who locked eyes with me for a moment and nodded. I returned the greeting as a voice beside me spoke with deep and confidence almost inside my ear. "No date tonight?"

I turned and looked up to see Twill, stepping out of the door just past the couple entering. He walked up and slipped into the iron lawn chair across from me, smiled gave me nod and waited with a quizzical look on his face.

Muse

IF HIS TONE WAS LOUD ENOUGH to reach me from the door, the people at the other tables didn't seem to notice. Twill was tall, lanky with a sandy beard and wavy head that seemed to have no trouble combing itself into a wild frenzy. He waited for a moment watching me from across the table, not saying anything. Then he leaned back and made himself comfortable, placing his hands on his chest and interlacing his fingers. The position didn't look to be the most comfortable considering the furniture, but in seconds he relaxed, completely at ease. He glanced from one table to the next, took no notice of the reading boy, and smiled towards the couple who smiled back and nodded. He lingered for a moment on the boy and girl still in the midst of their nonsensical conversation, then turned back to me with the same quizzical look and waited.

He looked old and I stared back at his large head and big eyes observing me with deep penetrating blues'. I decided not to speak, partially because I was feeling a little belligerent with the loss of the big man and still frustrated with my writing tonight, besides he sat down uninvited, he should be the one to say something. So I turned away and let my eyes wander through the glass as the group that just entered sat down at a table. The boy who had spoken to Drover still looked a little smiley and out of sorts as the friends conversed.

Near the far corner was another small group, with a girl in bright red tennis shoes. She had a big toothy genuine smile that felt warm and good to see, but for some reason I was aware of a twinge of jealousy toward these people having such a good time as I watched. I have to admit, I never much cared for big toothy smiles, it always reminded me of cartoon horses neighing, but there are a few that work and well at that. Hers worked, so much so that I was repulsed if you can understand my sort of retardedness.

I stared hard through the glass at them, the boy and girl conversation outside faded and I felt myself move forward. The sensation was dreamy and strange in my stomachs pit, but I didn't fight it. I reached the glass and it dissolved. Suddenly I could hear the girl in the red shoes laughing with her friends as she explained that she forgot her mixer tonight and therefore the performance was going to be acoustic. Her friends don't seem to mind and they continued to laugh and gab about people and happenings within their group of familiars, until the girl picked up her guitar and I saw her toothy smile begin to drip.

A seriousness overcame her, and at the first strum across the six string a veil draped and the annoying, repulsive, lovely smile went and she with it. The girl in the red shoes began to play. She took us with her to a world of longing, hopeful love that many women speak or sing about. Lost avenues, found by torn addressments to past ravens. The unsung and unknown heroes who bless sneezes and tear up after they take you with a simple "Hello." The Adonis' in regular guy bodies, willing to kick glass from your path and stand up for honor though embarrassment could be eminent.

She began to sing and the lights suddenly dimmed a little. The mood inside the room changed to something much different than her song's pitch and tempo, but almost imperceptibly the girl in the red shoes shifted key and voice and the effect was awesome. A few more people entered Pantheons and stepped up to the counter, but every mind was on the girl in the red shoes, transported.

From behind the bar the manager looked and threw me a smile that wasn't friendly, but familiar. It set a chill upon me and I shrunk before her. Though I had seen her I was certain I had never met her before, but it was as if this woman knew me, full and intimate. There was something malevolent and unnerving about her as if in the second she saw me, she knew everything there was to know, and in that moment I understood that she knew and saw more than anyone anywhere should. Stolen in the contact of a blink and thrown back as a violated emptiness. Every time I came here she was here. In fact, I suddenly realized, the regulars: the manager, Drover, the gypsy woman by the counter, the English looking guy who sat statuesque as he read, and Twill who still hadn't told me his name of course I hadn't asked for it, they were all always here. No matter the time or the day they were always here. I don't know why this fact unnerved me and I began to wonder of I was correct in my assumption.

My musings in and over the musical atmosphere of want and longing brought me to a memory of Thom Snell, who once was a friend of mine. It is an unfortunate thing that I must stress the was.

Thom was the 'Prince of Libation' and a fantastic poet. He spoke in a low monotone voice, called everyone "man" and used terms like "chick" and "motherfucker" as if they were second nature. Some people can't curse, it just isn't for everyone, they aren't comfortable or their voice isn't right for it. The same goes for displays of anger or yelling. Thom wasn't a loud brash yeller and didn't display a lot of anger. He loved Walter Mosley and got me to read a few of his books, but I never thought Thom was gullible enough to get sucked into the drama between some friends and I who, on an evening of extra curricular mind-expanding-chemical-alteration, got it in their heads that I was some sort of nark. And when a being is in an altered state like that, once they return from it, certain knowledge false or true may remain twisted permanently. Thusly they convinced Thom of their newfound knowledge. I didn't think Thom would follow the paranoia, but his world conspiracy theories, without any government love lost, probably aided his convincing.

But before all of that Thom was a friend, wonderful with words and bits of philosophy mixed in his aged knowledge from the sixties. "I knew this girl once," he said one evening with all of us standing outside a coffee shop just a few miles from where I found myself now. "She was so sweet, so beautiful, you couldn't help but fall in love with her just a little bit."

The girl in the red shoes, I suddenly realized, repulsed me for just that reason. I was not apart of her group of friends. I didn't know her and she didn't look at me in that way. She probably had a boyfriend, which always seems to be the way of things. In that sense I am taken to remembrances of numerous "ones" who have filled my sleepless nights with questions of possibility and wondering ifs. Friends and acquaintances passing by in fleeting conversations recited word for moment, trying to bridge the gaps of thousand year connections.

Life still cannot tell me what it was that caused such a churn of emotions, which left me breathless, with the want to ask questions that should have been voiced then.

Perhaps it was their smile, warm and real, speaking volumes to secret inner depths, making the child inside giggle in the anticipation. Perhaps it was their eyes, a magical beacon to a fellow time traveler to join the journey along the beaches of destiny to mountaintops of fate.

It is those feelings, which reach beyond the common animal physicality of carnal knowledge that takes you to another place, where time holds no bounds and spirits are endless. In those moments of fleeting opportunity there is always time enough for second and third chances to meet that someone more exotic, but instead, questions remain.

I heard someone once tell a story of a perfect rose growing in a lone field waiting to be picked by a lover. Deep crimson and long stemmed without a barb to be seen. But a single hidden thorn pricked, brings the trickle of red and its unconditional love was lost and with it life and holder passed it by to wither.

There is a room inside we venture into to heal wounds from lovers past. True love put away on a dusty shelf in the back of the mind, held in pictures, murals and sculptures, awaiting little things to be added. Imperfections polished and every curved nuance memorized.

Does anyone recall speaking to those lost phantasms?

Those who thought to save sanity and remove pain by turning their backs to the unknown, now stare into the mirror at three am laughing in the stupidity of loss.

Remember the stories of those most perfect ones' recanted by fear, when life's immortality was snatched, leaving all others to be held in comparison, even in the resplendent tone perfection. The inner self remains broken and left to its tortured end.

For the next two hours the girl in the red shoes sang, her voice airy and clear in her acoustic folk sound as she emoted heart written tales of life trials.

In the breaks she joked and laughed with friends that I also began to detest, but her smile, out, full of sincerity and joy…I decided to buy a CD just to hope and remember.

Stranger

"PRETTY GIRL."

At the sound of Twill's voice I was yanked back through the glass and suddenly found myself sitting in my chair. The feeling was sudden, ripped from the comfort of my own curiosity aborted. I turned towards Twill, staring at me as if he hadn't taken his eyes off. "What?" I asked still shocked and bewildered.

"Nothing, I was just commenting on your look. Admiring her."

I ignored him and turned back inside to the girl in the red shoes still playing. Something didn't make sense. Hadn't she finished a while ago? I remember her thanking everyone for coming out, putting her guitar away. She started laughing with her friends again as a few people bought copies of her CD. I even bought one and she smiled at me when I asked her to sign it. I checked my watch, it was still early, but I had watched her play for two hours. How could it still be early? I noticed something on the table in front of me, half hidden beneath a napkin. The CD I had purchased with her signature on the inside flap. "But that..."

"Is exactly what happened."

I looked across to Twill who held me with an amused grin.

"Problem?"

"No, not really." I was sarcastic.

"Okay." he shrugged and turned away.

I was a little confused. My memory told the truth of what I believed and yet here I was, back where I began, sitting outside and staring at the girl in the red shoes, exactly as I remembered her two hours ago. I stood, walked over to the door and opened it to listen for a moment. "Why is whyyyyyyy..." I let the door close. I remembered her singing that song and my head spun in an undefined luminescence. The girl in the red shoes closed her eyes and opened her mouth wide to all the expressed feeling the song conveyed.

I returned to my seat ignoring Twill who seemed to be watching me for some sort of reaction. As Twilight Zones' go, it always seemed sort of fun when this kind of thing happens to a character...or when it happens to me. Yes, this kind of thing has happened to me before, believe it or not, this type of literal déjà vu that truly interferes with reality and causes you to loose time and such. I no longer allow my self the fortitude to question, even though I don't completely understand it. I also don't pretend a bland absentee to the weirdness like so many others. Rather I relish it in the hope that I will eventually gain a greater knowledge along with some sort of clarity and understanding over what exactly is going on when this occurs. At the very least it helps hold me in the belief that, "There are more things in heaven and earth..."

Most people live in denial. I find myself right in the middle of the road, considered among the conservative/liberal minority who accepts and knows and by my understanding, I am allowed every so often to glimpse another succulent truth within the skein of the divine comedy. That said. I have never had anything like this overtake me so strongly or for so long, and I have never come through it with something I could hold and possess as irrefutable proof.

The front door opened and a few people exited, "Why is why..." one of the girls sang loudly off key, opening her mouth wide and shutting her eyes as she imitated the girl in the red shoes with feigned expressions of passion. Her friends all laughed.

In my life I have seen people playing at passion and usually they can be easily spotted. Just as the ones filled with it can be openly told because so much leaks from them by speech and action. Artists, the good ones anyway, and by good I mean true, have no recourse and are unable to help how and sometimes when it is expressed. The girl in the red shoes expressed her songs, felt the words and allowed emotion to drip from her tongue as electricity shot by her fingertips. She breathed and released it as her face contorted and her mouth opened wide to give herself to the audience and draw the oohs' and ahas' out for everyone to understand, as she became her voice.

The small group laughed again as the girl continued. "Why is wh…aaack..." She stopped walking and grabbed her throat. "Aaaack."

"Roxanne what's wrong, Roxanne?"

"I think she's choking!"

"Help her!"

"Hit her back!"

"Heimlich!" One of the guys grabbed her around the waist, but it was unnecessary.

"Aaaack, 'cough' 'cough'."

"Is she alright?"

"You alright Roxie?"

The girl coughed something up and spat. She nodded and her friends stepped back.

As this scene unfolded not ten feet from me, my attention was drawn back inside the glass to the counter where the manger stood staring at the girl cold and direct. Her face held only determination and when the group finally moved on with the girl now silent, her concentration broke and she returned to her tasks.

Twill had turned to watch the group with a sad half smile, "Jealousy," he said almost to himself, "can be cruel thing and bring about some unfortunate results." He fell silent again. His constant vague narrative was a little unnerving.

"What?" I said turning to him with a little more annoyance in my voice than I believed I should have.

Twill's face still held the smirk as he turned to me, "Do you think people bring on the things they don't like in their lives?"

Were we having a conversation? Twill's sudden question threw me back and I was not certain how to answer. "What?" I asked again realizing I was starting to sound like an idiot.

Twill locked eyes with me, "I said, is it a persons contention that brings on the negative happenings in his or her life, or is it fate, or do you simply believe that there is no order at all, and things just simply happen, completely void of any sort of influence, irreverent or divine?"

Now I heard it, and what did he mean? I had no idea. "Is this a trick question?"

Twill smiled again and sat back returning his attention to the patrons inside. The gypsy was sitting at her table just beneath the counter. She noticed Twill looking and smiled giving him a slight nod. "She can "see" you know."

I looked at the old woman. I always liked looking at her whenever I was here. She looked kind and reminded me of my grandmother of she were still alive. She didn't look like her or anything, in fact quite the opposite. The gypsy woman was tiny, frail, and the few times I remember seeing her move from that seat, she used a knotted old cane and walked hunched, but she had a welcoming smile that somehow lit the room and brightened the day of anyone happening by her. A small round face, button nose and kind eyes, but I would never get my palm read by her. The woman was on a pedestal in my mind and I didn't want to bring her down from that for some palmist novelty.

"They say she has power."

I didn't look at Twill. I wondered what his real name was. His constant interjections were both welcoming and got on my nerves. "So she's read your palm?" I decided to throw little back at him.

His voice chuckled, "No. No I don't think so. Besides there wouldn't be anything to read."

I turned. Twill wasn't looking at me. Just an old man relaxing in his chair, staring into the shop, aged, wizened. I figured he was right. Maybe he was sick or dying or just done. There wouldn't be anything left for someone like him. Twill had probably been through "it", all of it, and didn't need a palm reader telling him a bunch of shit he already knew.

"You should check it out." He said.

"Maybe later..."

Twill shrugged. "So what brings you out on this night?"

My mind flashed and shut down. There was a tone to his question that had implications, though I was uncertain as to what they were and I suddenly realized I had no idea how I arrived here tonight. I looked down both sides of the street. My car was not out front. Down the street? Perhaps. My eyebrows curled. How the hell did I get here? And why had I come?

I opened my mouth to speak thinking it would just emerge on its own, but nothing came out.

Twill smiled. "It's okay, it happens. Pantheons holds itself to an open, family oriented atmosphere." He shrugged. "Fact is, you might not want to remember. It can be quite troublesome at times. So much that you might not want to leave."

I found his words somewhat humorous and decided to blow of the comment, but the not remembering did send a bit of trepidation down my spine. I thought harder, streets flashed, my car, I ate, and I was at home at one point… something weird happened I think, something curious… a little scary? I felt the hairs on my neck rise as a bit of awareness crept back in. Where was I anyway? I recognized the coffee shop…or did I? Pantheons. Why was I so confused all of a sudden? My head felt foggy. I ate something that made me sick. I heard Twill's question again and it echoed in my head. His voice had a different tone. I looked up into the coffee shop again and everything looked different, as if I had never seen it before. The regulars had an air about them and…

"Don't worry about it." Twill's voice called and brought me back from the faraway and everything stopped. I forgot what I was wondering about and settled into the iron seat to let time pass.

Taken

SITTING OUTSIDE PANTHEONS across from Twill was intoxicating for reasons I could not readily explain, and when I released my mind to go, I ventured through the glass for hours on end and back, each time finding that almost no time had passed. The only moment I found it unpleasant and upsetting was when I crossed the English looking man that sat inside at a table near the window. He was constantly reading with a steaming cup of tea beside his completely unassuming demure, and he gave no attention to anyone. It was his lack of interest that interested and disturbed me. The night wore on, the coffee shop grew louder, chattering over the girl in the red shoes playing through their own conversations, but the English looking man didn't seem to notice and when I dared approach, focusing directly on him or the book he was reading for more than a few seconds, I was violently thrown back outside into my chair beside Twill.

The first time it happened I spoke some sort of expletive like "shit", "fuck" of "fucking shit."

"Yeees!" Twill said drawing the word out long and matter-of-factly.

It struck me so fast and with such intensity, my chest seized and the wind was knocked out of me. I couldn't breathe and I shut my eyes choking. I was able to expel a cough once then my left arm went numb as the pressure on my chest increased. A hand suddenly lay on my chest and my body relaxed. My normal breathing suddenly returned and all my struggling ceased and for some reason my breathing felt much more open and easier than it did before. I opened my eyes to Drover standing over me, one of his hands on my chest and staring into my eyes with such gentle open kindness I was overcome and instinctively bowed my head. He removed his hand and placed them together in prayer, closed his eyes and dropped his head low. The skin on the backs of his hands had two dark spots like cancerous scars. I placed my hands together and closed my eyes as well. When I opened them, there was no trace of Drover before me. I found him sitting on the brick flower box in front of the hair salon again, staring at me as if he hadn't moved.

I clutched my chest and took a deep clear breath. "What the fuck was that?"

"What indeed." Twill answered. "Don't be so nosey. Some people don't like it."

"Yes, but…"

"It's a comedy."

"What is?"

"The book the Englishman's reading, it's a comedy. Excuse me a moment." Twill said standing. He moved towards the door and I can't say what happened next, because a moment later Twill was sitting back in his chair again. I didn't remember him returning, he was just back as if he had never left...

On the other side of the glass things were definitely different. A guy and a girl were now sitting at the gypsy's table, the girl in the red shoes was taking a break and her friends were all talking again. There were new people in the shop and some had left. What the hell happened? I checked my watch, but the hands were reading like a Dali-esque painting and I couldn't discern what they meant.

"Now that was a little different wasn't it?"

It was Twill speaking I think, but the voice was far away. My head was light again and filled with cotton, I couldn't focus on anything around me, but it seemed that my mind could comprehend more clearly than before. Everything about me, my life, who I was, where I was, even how I got here suddenly became evident. All new information was suddenly off limits like where the hell here was. I remember feeling like this during certain drug-induced escapades, as if everything around had readily stepped out of a dream and I found myself... questioning my self.

Am I apart of this or is it apart of me?

Sleep deprived hallucinations are fun, but can be somewhat terrifying, especially when you are driving. Your pupils dilate, shadows seem to walk, while walls and images melt in your eyes. Lights and spots seem to attach to your sight and move wherever you look. I'm near sighted so at that point when things are at their most surreal, I can take off my glasses and allow the show to really begin. Shapes in daylight begin move on their own allowing the mind to believe whatever it wants.

Unlicensed hallucination.

These bouts, within the context of your extremities can begin on your uncaffinated second or twentieth wind on the fourth day after you have gone without any real sleep. Anyone brave or stupid enough to push into the fifth day, be prepared, because even now the mind begins too detach itself from the walls of reality. The sensation of touch begins separate from the mind and there is no sense of I. What you do touch feels as if "the you" is touching someone else or someone is touching "the you". Reality starts to loose its cohesion as the mind starts to jell and split, confused buy the dream state it is attempting to get into. The secret to getting here is eating minimally, and drinking lots of water.

Blinking takes forever because whenever you shut your eyes they truly don't want to open again. I am quite positive it looks funny because my friends were laughing at me, as was my girlfriend, because whatever you are saying is not being said to them, but to the dream creatures dancing through your mental frame.

Second winds arrive at regular intervals, every fifteen to thirty minutes, and you feel like you're fine and can stay up for the rest of the day. This sensation only lasts for three to five minutes. When you blink and try to open your eyes, your head moves upward in the direction you want your lids to go, but your lids remain closed. Your head tilts all the way back, because at this point the lids' need leverage to open and when they do, they rise heavy from the serene comfort of being shut. If you are outside when this occurs be careful because the sun at this point seems to have gone supper nova. It hurts and your eyes quickly shut again. At which point it is best to just rub them and help them up with your fingers. This activity repeats itself as you time travel through your day from wind to wind.

I know of no person that has gone into the fifth day though it must delve into some serious levels of damage. I heard it said that theoretically anyone that stays awake for a solid week would be completely insane.

Recovery for attempting my bit of stupidity is about three to four days of rest.

Though highly enlightening and something to tell stories about later on, sleep deprivation is terrifying when you're in the middle of it and wrought with unreal levels of paranoia. There are other things that grant these communion-like experiences that teeter on the surreal, but the ones coming from the everyday unexplained are undoubtedly the most rewarding. I have found myself in the midst of things which both physically and mentally I couldn't possibly have achieved without some sort of outside influential aid.

I once made a pencil move with my mind, had a book jump off the shelf into my hands, changed the channel without the remote. I have predicted births' and deaths', known and intercepted people in obscure places out of necessity. Now I am aware that millions of others do these things as well, though many of those people dismiss all of these instances as coincidence. The difference between a few others that I have had the great fortune of coming across and myself, versus the rest of the world is that we don't deny it. We allow for the constant possibility and try to make it happen again and again. And, we are successful.

Coincidence is something people say just to mask their fear of the unknown.

Socrates

"NICE COUPLE," Twill said. I still didn't know his name. He was staring at a man and woman sitting with the gypsy. I didn't remember them coming in. Twill looked proud. "So?" he turned to me.

"So what?"

"What do you think?" he nodded back through the glass at the couple.

This was becoming frustrating.

"You think so?"

"What?"

"You think this is becoming frustrating?"

I looked at him. He didn't turn but remained focused inside. "I didn't say that."

"No, you didn't say that. What's your point?"

"So you read minds. Is that some little trick you do just to mess with people?"

"Does it mess with you?"

"Do you always speak in riddles?" I asked the question to throw a little of him, back at him.

Twill smiled. "Alright, now you're beginning, finally. Do you have a problem with riddles?"

"What sort of riddles are we speaking of? Who's on first, what's on second?"

"And Idon'tknow is on third, but that point was made years ago. What's yours?"

I thought for a second. "Must I have a point and if so why is it so important to you?"

Twill flinched, either by the question or just by me asking one, he flinched, but only for a second. "We all have points, ours or others, but points we have. There is a point to everything, whether we know it or not, isn't there? There is a reason for everything and coincidence is something people say just to mask their fear of the unknown."

Now it was my turn to flinch.

Twill continued. "The importance of your point to me is negligible and truly unimportant. My questions are merely an attempt at your personal realization, once you begin thinking of course, and leave the external and delve into the infinite space that is you. Humph... Man thinks space is the final frontier, when there are infinite levels within which can make "spaces" so much easier to explore and understand." He turned back to the shop interested and I followed his gaze.

The Englishman reading by the window was looking up. I could never remember him moving a muscle much less looking up. I never saw him get his tea, a refill, or even turn a page. He was staring at the couple sitting with the gypsy and as I watched, the atmosphere beyond the glass shifted. From the gypsy and the couple I felt...love was it? Whatever it was, it was overwhelming, calm and tangible and though I was staring at their backs, I felt, anyone looking would know this couple was in love.

A moment ago the Englishman filled me with a chilling level of dread and suddenly I felt it again, much stronger than before. The girl in the red shoes was situated between them still playing her concert and from my view it looked as if the light inside suddenly became considerably darker on the Englishman's side than the other.

I was outside, but the conflicted emotions seemed to spill out onto the street. Behind the bar the manager looked up and in the corner of my eye I saw Drover look in my direction and stand. Inside some of the patrons began glancing around the room at each other, anxious. The girl in the red shoes made a mistake in her playing and made a joke. People laughed but the tone on the room remained uneasy and they continued to look around.

The Englishman at the table stood. The gypsy reached over and took the couples hands in hers as she spoke to them. I wondered if she felt it too.

The light flickered for a moment and I thought I saw the gypsy move, but it was in a flash, fast and unclear, maybe it was just her hands though she was holding onto the couple.

Suddenly the lights returned to normal and the Englishman was sitting back in his seat, book in hand, and locked in his regular position as if nothing had occurred. All the patrons, along with the girl in the red shoes went back to their business. The gypsy spoke to the couple and Drover was back on the flower box again.

"Rasha!" Twill said reverently nodding his head and turning back to me. "Once she makes up her mind she can be quite an adversary."

"Rasha?"

"The seer."

"The palm reader?"

"The seer. Rasha does not read palms nor does she interpret the Tarot. She sees, and she speaks."

It did occur to me at this point that I was completely engaged in conversation with Twill and yes it unnerved me a little because I didn't ask for this, he had simply invited himself to sit, done so and engaged me.

"What is your name?" I asked. The question came out of frustration before I even thought about it.

Twill smiled broadly, "No."

"No?"

"No, that isn't the question you want to ask. No, you're not ready for the answer. And no, I'm not telling you because you already know."

These riddles were becoming sort of fun. I accepted at this point that I was not going to get any information from Twill that he didn't want to give and as he continued talking he gave me what he wanted so there was no reason to ask him anything…

"Exactly." He said.

I wasn't even going to try to go after that one.

"I'll tell you what. If you can tell me how you got here, I will tell you my name."

That sounded fair and easy enough, I was just thinking about it. Unfortunately it turned out to be quite a task… Whenever I tried to focus, my mind went blank. I looked up the street again. Where was my car? Inside the glass, the couple stood up from Rasha's table. They looked so happy it was sickening.

The Englishman reading by the window watched them as they passed. His face had a scornful look, so intense, I felt ill. It seemed that he and I were the only two who didn't welcome the union.

The couple stepped out the front door and I noticed the bag the man was carrying and suddenly realized it was the Reading Kid. I hadn't even seen him get up and he didn't have a girl with him, did he? Where did she come from? And the bag he was carrying looked light and the book he had was thick, it didn't look as if he had it with him.

It didn't take me long to find the thing, sitting of all places, on the table beside Rasha. What the hell?

"Beautiful isn't it, new love, burgeoning romance. Would you care to take a guess at their future?"

"What do you mean?"

"I always find it interesting to try and guess the outcome of situations, couples, romance, arguments, what have you. Things as simple or as vast as spilling coffee or even getting married."

"Well they look happy to me."

"Looks can be deceiving, but since Rasha was involved I'd say their odds are considerably good." He turned to me. "You aren't even going to try? It isn't like you haven't done it before."

Beneath Wind

"I DON'T MAKE PREDICTIONS ABOUT LOVE."

"At all or anymore?"

I looked at Twill eyeing me as faces flashed in my head. I had memories of two, no three of them, always the same. Once the reminiscing on these is dismissed, I begin to recall the lesser she-demons that plague my memory.

There are those affairs, which we cannot speak of outside of historical context, and some can hold a great deal of pain within their memory. They are not demons of course, but only buy digging to the bottom of a soup pot do you find what's really in it. The truth of most of the flavors, whether or not it's been burned and once all if that has been stirred, the flavor changes and you really know what you have.

Twill's question felt like a direct stab at my depth and as the memories surfaced I became defensive. I decided not to answer.

"Pride." He exhaled. "You know it has destroyed civilizations."

I turned to him and nodded.

"You know," I said. "I have found that as good a judge of character as I am, I cannot make those determinations for myself and since no one has come to give me aid nor taken the advise they have asked me for, I would just as soon leave people to their own judgments."

"You know, a long time ago." Twill began. "There was a bird the likes of which you have never seen and certainly would not believe. Its wingspan was nearly twelve feet at full extension, with the most brilliant yellow/white feathers that made you think of gold when it reflected in the sunlight. It had a long neck, always reared back majestically and when a flock flew overhead it would silence all the animals in the forest. So beautiful were these birds that they were worshiped in many corners around the world, more so than the Egyptian felines. It was this pride and worship that would turn out to be its undoing, for at that same time, the Pegasus were also flying, also worshiped, much less than the great birds, but there were rumblings, thoughts which began to believe that quite possibly, the Pegasus, creatures of both land and sky must surely be the greatest creatures on all the world. It was the wanton majesty of the wingless Horses on land and the winged Pegasus in the air that caused such stir in the world.

"A resentful foulness crept into the great birds. It seemed they had been favored, with their brilliant feathers and long neck, for the Pegasus were not as you see them in mythology, beautiful and white, no. They were just as you see the horses running today. Palomino, chestnut, gray, white and black, certainly bold and yes beautiful with intelligence as the day was long and I dare say no prideful obsession.

"The great birds didn't believe the Pegasus should be worshiped. They believed the winged mutations of the horse, which stretched to forty feet from tip to tip, were far too big to be in the sky and should stick to the ground. So, one day a group of the large birds was elected to call upon the gods to aid them."

At the mention of "the gods", I looked at Twill curiously. He didn't seem to notice and continued the story.

"After years of unanswered pleading and supplication, one god did answer their prayers and the group of birds was summoned to Hades."

I eyed him again.

"Yes, Hades." Twill answered the unasked question. "And Hades asked the great birds what it is they have been praying about for so long? The birds conveyed their displeasure about the Pegasus and how unfair it was to have these land creatures, *obviously land creatures,* flying in their air. They called it their air because all creatures gave way when they flew by. All creatures except the Pegasus."

"What would you have me do?" Hades asked.

"Take away their wings." The birds cried. *"Strike them down."*

"Hades could easily do this without permission even though Zeus had created the Pegasus himself, but Hades' meddling would surely infuriate the king of the gods. The last thing Hades wanted was to start an all-out war with Zeus whom the other gods would easily side. Hades would be fighting endlessly.

"I must consider this." Hades said. *"You are welcome to wait."*

"The great birds didn't wish to linger within the heated pits of flaming wrath around them, but they were elected to find a solution to the problem. They had to remain for bird pride.

"Hades wasn't about to cower before Zeus asking for permission to strike down his precious Pegasus. So instead, he went to the Horses and explained the situation to them. The Horses didn't care one way or another, but Hades had a bargain for them. In exchange for helping to convince the Pegasus too give up their wings he will give the Horses the ability to speak. The Horses were very intrigued by this and could not resist the chance to communicate directly with men on an equal level. They had thoughts and opinions and were never listened to, so the advantages of speech far outweighed the ability to fly.

"So the horses agreed and with a little coaxing the Pegasus agreed as well, speech for wings was surely profound. So behind Zeus' back, Hades informed the other gods of the willing bargain he had struck with the Horses and the Pegasus.

"Hades returned to hell seven days later and summoned the great birds. The time in hell had taken its toll. Their bodies were now blackened with soot, their long necks were pasty and the brilliant yellow/white nearly golden feathers were unrecognizable.

"Hades smiled. *"I agree to what you wish."* Then his face

turned with an evil sneer that intimidated the birds and had them wishing to be back home as soon as possible. *"The Pegasus will loose their wings,"* Hades proclaimed. *"And all will become horses and you shall all be exactly as you are now."* Hades shook his head in worry. *"I shall certainly be defending myself from Zeus for this bargain. All the other Gods will go to war with me, but do you agree to what I have said?"* The birds all quickly agreed, anxious to have the bargain set so they would be able to leave.

"Hades smiled and even escorted the great birds to the gates where they flew back to the flock with the wonderful news.

At that very moment all the Pegasus, but Zeus' own, landed all over the earth, never to fly again and at that same moment there was a painful cry from the great nests and caves around the world.

"We should stop and bathe." One of the Great birds said on their journey back. "Arrive majestically before the others."

"No, this soot and grime is proof that we went on our journey and returned, we shall all be heroes with stories told of us for years to come."

"The birds flew into the cave of the great counsel of birds and landed before the others. Every great bird waiting before them was covered with soot and grime, looking very woeful and very angry.

"WHAT HAVE YOU DONE?" they cried.

"The great birds looked at one another confused. *"We went to Hades and made a bargain. The Pegasus no longer has their wings and we shall be the greatest birds in the sky. Why are you all covered with soot?"*

"We are covered with nothing, this is how we awoke. This happened last night. Just as the Pegasus were landing wingless, we became this. What did you bargain?"

"The birds were confounded. "Nothing. Hades said he agreed to what we requested. The Pegasus would loose their wings and we… we would… all stay… exactly as we are now."

"Exactly as we were then." One of the others said, his head and long neck dropping in sorrow.

"The Vultures suddenly realized their mistake and what Hades meant by his words. He referred to the birds standing before him, their beautiful coats blacked by the fires of hell. For seven days they ate the only food they could find which were things dying or already dead and that memory also carried through all the great birds, The Carrion Birds as they were to be known after that day.

"Zeus was furious, but after learning the Pegasus had agreed he calmed and kept his own steed.

"The horses relished in their newfound speech and the drunken confusion of that, resulted in the creation of the Centaur race, but that is a story for another time."

"You know I don't want to be rude," I spoke up once Twill was done and the sarcasm in my voice was a little thick. "What the hell does that have to do with anything at all?"

Twill smiled. "That's for you to decide. What do you take from it?"

"It's mythology."

"Is it?"

"Yes, but I've never heard that story."

"Have you heard about the horses throat?"

"No."

"That it is believed they once had the ability to speak?"

"That doesn't even make sense. Whatever. Okay so why can't they speak anymore?"

"The story goes on to say Hades was good on his bargain, all the horses could speak, however, none of their offspring had the ability to do so."

"And I am supposed to get something out of that story?"

"No."

"No?"

"As I said it's up to you." Twill sat back in his chair.

"The story is about pride and jealously. And don't make a bargain with the devil unless you've analyzed every word."

"But even the analysis of every word can be changed, re-construed by their definition."

"So don't deal with the devil at all?"

Twill didn't respond.

Gloaming

EPISODES OF THE TWILIGHT ZONE are filled with those kinds of lessons. Retold mythologies of what happens to those who try to make a deal with the devil. Of course every so often, someone outsmarts him, "Devil came down to Georgia" and all that. I like stories of average men outsmarting timeless riddles of the universe. The most difficult riddle I know goes like this: You're standing before two unmarked doors; one door leads to life, the other to death. Standing before each door is a person, one always lies and one always tells the truth. You may only ask one question. What is the one question you can ask both of them that will tell you which door to go through?

I always enjoyed riddles until I came across that one. It's the wording that makes it a riddle and you must analyze the words and try to figure out how to deconstruct the riddle, in this case it's "both of them." Science fiction is the only genre that truly allows freedom with riddles, pushing possibility beyond good verses evil and love concurs all and nothing took science fiction to its absolute limit, better than the Zone, which was the launch pad for most of the science fiction and horror of today.

It was still early. The transposition of time kept things fresh and didn't allow me to miss anything. The story Twill told only took a minute of real time. If I had the presence to question any of the evening thus far, I was afraid to, believing it would all end. The words he spoke were illuminating and I could picture the scenes in my mind.

Two girls stepped out of the coffee shop and sat at the table where the smoking kid had been. My first thought was where did they come from. They were cute, there was no way I could have missed them entering. They were giggly, but not stupid and sat down with their drinks keeping to their conversation. Both gave me a cursory glance in turn and I smiled. One smiled back, the one I was interested in did not. That figures.

It is strange to imagine my relationship with my father is a corollary to my relationships with women. I often find my mother staring back at me from the eyes of the women I date. The look isn't sexual or codling, but I get the feeling it's how my mother views my father in a sort of surrogate, protect me daddy way. It is said we all marry our parents, but when I see that look, I am reminded of the lack of communication and arguing I always saw between them. I feel that if I stay, I will inevitably become my father so I take it as my cue to leave. All women attracted to me seem to have father issues of abandonment or unavailability. By that rational they must see in me an abandoning or unavailable persona, which makes me nervous, because that must be what I am if it is what I am projecting.

"What is the question?" Twill sounded a little frustrated.

"What question?"

"The question you're supposed to ask the two standing at the doors?"

It was my turn and I couldn't resist. I smiled and looked inside the coffee shop, ignoring him.

The two kids that needed to be slapped finally finished their discussion about life and got up to leave. Two guys preparing to enter Pantheons stepped back and took the table. A moment later one of them got up and went inside.

"You're not going to tell me?" Twill asked.

"Do you want me to tell you?" I asked.

Twill smiled and I saw a father's pride, as a prodigy that had come so far.

I don't have a very good relationship with my father. I'm sure that's no big surprise. I haven't known many who do and an acceptable relationship of dysfunction does not count. Because of that I have always tended to gravitate towards father figures, but older now I must say I truly understand what's behind his actions.

The other day I saw a man in an office answer his phone. He was about my age, bigger and he had that other something I don't have, a grownupness stemming from family responsibility weighting everything against what needs to be done first.

I couldn't hear the conversation he was having, it was a little intense. He hung up the phone and dialed again.

"Why haven't you called? … It's been two hours since you got home. ... Do you have any homework? … How's your science grade?"

I shrunk at the sound of the question, intimidated by this man who had nothing to do with me, who was not my father and hell I wasn't even in school.

"No... No... No I just talked to your teacher."

I always wondered on that one because it always seemed like my father had esp. or something and this guy let his kid off the hook early, which derailed any sort of lying that would end up burying him. His son I'm certain didn't know how lucky he was. The father wasn't angry or loud, but I knew he could get there.

"We will be talking when I get home."

My shoulders got tight as I sat on the other side of the phone listening to my dad speak to me.

"But you wont be doing anything until that grade comes up. Nothing, no bike, no games, no television, nothing."

It was déjà vu as my past arrived by an alternate timeline.

He said goodbye and hung up, and when he turned I could see the utter disappointment on his face. This man released a long sigh and I suddenly saw something in him I'm certain was in my father, but I had never been on this side before. Not like this. And the way it was handled... doesn't matter. It has been over two decades and I finally understand.

It's the want for your offspring to wind up better than you. To know that it is possible for them if they would just work a little bit and try a little harder and the disappointing fear that they would not and follow your path.

"Would you say that makes everything alright or at least better?" Twill asked.

I no longer felt the need to question Twill's comments and responses. It was obvious he was somehow connected to my musings. Reading my mind sounds corny. "I understand him more," I said. "His actions might have been out of fear for me, his way of educating, beating and screaming lessons into me by some absurdness in him that made it necessary. He wasn't wrong or evil, yet he tries to believe and make everyone else believe he doesn't remember any of it."

"Does he?"

"He does. He might deny the details, but he does. I believe I have made my peace with it and now I'm in the process of putting it behind me and finding my place in it all."

"Then it is alright?"

"Yes," I thought about it. "Except when it's not."

Twill nodded.

I stared at the old man sitting across from me for full minute, watching him watch people. "If I ask the him which one is the door to life, what will he say? Whatever one you ask that question to, you know the answer is the opposite door."

Twill thought about it. "Because one always lies to the opposite of the truth and one always tells the truth to the liar's lie about the opposite?"

"Exactly."

"Hum. That is hard."

I turned to the window waiting for what I was certain to come next.

"I know a harder one though."

& Found

"WHAT ARE YOU DOING HERE?" Twill asked after a long interval of silence, where I watched the couple in the corner silently arguing through the glass. The argument was about the girl in the red shoes. She was friendly and amid the friendly gestures of a particular song, the girl saw something, became jealous began to make accusations. I knew this because I had witnessed it a few times already. Through the glass, time moved forward, but in my return it was always back to the moment I moved into the glass.

The question from Twill sounded rhetorical, but I turned to see him staring at me with a fierce gaze. I looked for the joke or question in his eyes as I began to stammer over my response, "Well…I…" His eyebrow twitched and I waited, but he didn't blink. He wasn't going to let me off, though my head was completely blank as to the answer.

"Why are you here?"

Images suddenly sprang to mind, a man bigger than any man I'd ever seen, other strange people, happenings and…

"The question isn't that difficult!" Twill's tone was sharp and sounded a little annoyed. His gaze didn't waver. "I can't believe a person such as yourself…"

I blinked.

"Yes you!" Twills tone was sarcastic and shockingly loud. He leaned across the table. "You sit there complacent and superior, having learned to read people outside of the norm, which you believe is supposed to make you unique and special, but you fail to understand, special cannot exist in a bubble!"

I was shocked into a submissive quiet by his tone along with the sudden realization that no one heard what had been said. Everyone just went about their conversations as Twill continued to berate me.

"So by that, and your personal belief that you are better, I ask you, what the fuck are you doing here, and you can't answer so simple a query. How is that what you pretense?"

I was getting angry, but I kept my tone calm, "pretense?"

"Yes pretense, better than everyone else."

The conversation suddenly felt somewhat familiar by its angry one-sided tone, I tried to remain calm. "Why are you telling me this?"

"WHAT ARE YOU DOING HERE?"

"I don't know what the I'm doing here okay!" I yelled back. Everyone outside turned towards me and some inside turned to stare out through the glass as well. Twill sat smugly back in his seat as I felt my face suddenly flush.

'Man is the only animal that blushes, or needs to.' I thought. Samuel Clemens was a great student of the human drama and condition, and I often recall that quote in embarrassing situations. I nodded my apologies mouthing 'sorry' to the couple, the men and the girls who wouldn't make eye contact with me, along with a few faces inside. The guiltless Twill kept the slight smirk on his face.

"And the point of that?" I think I spoke too softly to be heard, but Twill doubtless was reading my mind again.

"What do you think the importance of that was?"

"Getting me riled up so I could embarrass myself…?"

"Did you embarrass yourself?"

"No." I was frustrated and upset. "I don't want to do this anymore." I kept checking my peripheral to see if the girls looked up, especially the one I was interested in.

"No one knows what we are talking about and I can assure you no one really cares and is now back to his or her own business. Your belief that they are concerning themselves with you is the reality you perceive, whether or not it is a true reality, you make real in your mind and actions."

This was the most conclusive statement Twill had made all night. "Thoughts determine reality," I concluded. "And our reality is created by what we believe."

Twill made a move, which looked like a slight nod, but he turned back to the shop as he did, so I could have misinterpreted it.

My mind flashed again, "But my chosen interpretations are all that really matter in any situation..."

Twill nodded so slightly it was again missed and I considered for a moment. Yes he had nodded, by my perceptions I saw a nod, so yes it was.

"So," Twill's smugness had gone, replaced by the same person that sat across from me most of the night. "What have you learned at this point?"

Somehow I knew twill was speaking about my life in general and not me sitting here tonight.

"Your feeding and study only serve to feed and study, whether it is for enlightenment or complacency. Complacency is without practice, it is the lack of it and this is why you find no complaint or true restriction by things. Things which mean nothing. Those that may truly cause growth are often cast aside and/or devalued in many senses. Lately those things are being used for that purpose, to remove their value. You take the things and make them a vice."

I simply stared at Twill listening and understanding almost nothing about what he said. "You know if you speak in tongues people will only understand 'blah blah blahhhh'." He wasn't amused.

"The point you are missing is the responsibility that comes with the knowledge you sought and found for yourself."

"What responsibility?" the image came to my head as I spoke it and he didn't answer, he didn't need to, so he responded with another question.

"How many have you read?"

I thought about the image of books running through my mind. The "self helps", religious doctrines, philosophers, metaphysical bodies of work that seemed to literally leap off the shelf at me from time to time. And I kept reading and reading until the process became cyclical and knowledge began to come on its own. Words from my self or friends in everyday life, then life in general, guiding me to more awareness than I ever even imagined. My head spun faster with more imminence and I became aware of the coffee shop again. Pantheons. Tonight's patrons and the regulars, but there was some…thing about the regulars. Something unguarded though elusive. A depth that felt terrifying. There was something underlying in the Englishman reading by the window, the manager, Drover, the seer Rasha and Twill…

Donde Esta La Biblioteca de Alexandria

"DO YOU REMEMBER YOUR FIRST TRUTH?"

I thought to myself, venturing as far back as I could remember to high school, middle, elementary, even kindergarten, which in and of itself had been a severe rift in my reality, giving me my first experience of fear and being outcast for one reason or another. I was raised a bit coddled and as a result was taken aback back by rougher kids and as I grew up, found that Elementary was more of the same. A people grow and life happens things change, faiths are questioned leaving some lost as others are found. Some truths are recreated, but those discovered under direst are more tangible, and may never be lost.

Through all of those momentous happenings in my life, I can remember believing in everything.

I wasn't raised on "fiction." I don't ever remember ever being told what "story" was, and thereby in my youth I accepted all things as truth. Things that were fundamental to the institution of common knowledge, I questioned. Imagine growing up in a dream state of perpetual ecstasy where Santa Clause, monsters, cartoons and fantasy were all accepted as truths. In the reality of everyday, I understood and accepted all truths behind the fantastic and macabre, while still seeing many correlations between the so-called untruths. So my wisdom did nothing to stop my belief in possibility.

I was never afraid of clowns, probably because their connection to a humanistic persona could so readily be seen, but I was terrified of the giant characters walking around amusements parks. Horror films and dark empty rooms frightened me into high school. I could never explain these things, but my greatest confusion erupted though my religious upbringing.

If the life I was living was steeped in the rules of society, gravity, and physics, leaving everything outside of that to be considered a fictional untruth, then something in me took issue with bible stories. Many of the science fictional tales told on the Twilight Zone, mirrored biblical tales and had people with extraordinary abilities doing wondrous, albeit "unbelievable" things. My reasoning began to take all things into account, which led to a great deal of confusion because, for me, both realities were the same. Still, one was considered fact and the other fiction. I remember once in a high school religious debate an atheist said to me, *"If humans are so pretentious to believe that we have a soul, why doesn't everything else."* I thought about this statement for most of the semester until I finally determined, *"You're right, everything does have soul."*

They didn't like my answer.

So I accepted all with the understanding that I was not like as my hero's then, but one day… perhaps… Crazy?

"No."

I figured one day I would understand and… "What?" I said turning to Twill.

"I said no, to your question."

"You're not just asking questions anymore?"

"Would you like me to ask more questions?" Twill said slyly.

"I never really stopped believing as I grew up, you know. As if…"

"There are always possibilities."

"Yes exactly. I remember thinking that there was some underlying factor which connected everything and if I could just understand it, then everything would become clear." I turned to Twill. He seemed to be ignoring me again. "Society says the bible is real, but society, even religious society says all things that move in those "more than human" circles is unreal. There is a group out of the Vatican that investigates any so-called miracle, most likely to debunk it as they do. I suspect however, more often than not, people, including the Vatican, want the fictional to be true so then can get a firmer grip on God as a whole. So that they can believe even more."

Twill was smiling again, but he wasn't looking at me. "So your first truth was?"

I sat in blank silence for a moment, not thinking about anything, holding an empty dark space in my head. My thoughts wandered, I pulled them back again and again until I was certain then finally uttered, "Everything is true."

Twill smiled broadly and turned towards me, "Now, tell me about the book." he said standing.

He gestured me to stand and as I did so the coffee shop dissolved and I went blind.

I noticed that Drover, the manager and the seer Rasha, were all staring at me, even the man by the window seemed to glance up as the building melted into the pitch.

"Tell me of the book." Twill said in the darkness.

"The book?"

"Your truth, or should I say the book that became your truth."

Everything was set into blackness, my mind felt as if it was turning inside out. I was panicked and desperate to see. I couldn't feel anything, my limbs didn't exist and a deep cold began to swallow me. The image of the Englishman sitting at the table came to mind and I froze. He was staring at me and felt as if I was being taken or possessed by something. If there was air in this place, I wasn't aware of it until it was gone then I began to choke. My chest seized again, disembodied, no oxygen, no limbs and my eyes saw only darkness.

"Remember." Twill's voice released in a calming whisper all around me. "Just relax and remember the book. Think of your truth. Think of the book."

A dull light appeared, then a black book dispersed the darkness with a glow around it. I recognized it well having read the volume several times. On the binding across the top "the Razors Edge" embossed in gold letters. The pages were old and beginning to crack and the binding had been torn just a little as it corroded and starting to give. This was the most precious gift I had ever received from anyone, not the book, but its discovery and the lesson that came with it.

The character of Larry was, *"a very remarkable creature."*

"What are you doing tonight?" I remember my mother had called me out of the blue saying, "There's a movie I found. I saw it years ago and I want you to see it." I arrived at the house reluctantly and began to watch what I thought would be a most boring experience. She wouldn't tell me anything about it and when the television blazed in black and white, my disappointment was complete. I did pay attention however and not ten minutes later I was utterly absorbed by this story.

The book opened before me, the yellowed pages turned and I remembered my search for this out-of-print volume that I had begun to hunt for right after the movie ended. I finally found this copy, its anima glowing before me and I don't need to tell you the book was better, but the thing is it was so much better. And in reading it I discovered a strange mystery as whether or not the story was based on true events. The writer, Somerset Maugham placed himself in the book and maintains in a few places that the story is true.

"It gave me a strength I never possessed." In the darkness I spoke out loud though I couldn't feel my mouth.

"Why?" Twill's voice joined me.

"It held a profound truth muddled against the established norms."

"And as a result?"

"Result?"

"The result of this, your truth found in a volume, be it real or fictional. What was the result of that?"

"The entire thing turned out to be a grand connection for me, it remains the most interesting and concrete piece of advice I ever received from my mother. It began a search for knowledge and truth that has encompassed me ever since. It helped me find my place in the universe, wrought with all I understand and all we are told about how the world is and will be. It turned me away from a well-traveled road and I ended up on another with the belief that I was lost."

"And were you?"

"No."

"How do you know?"

"I know, because that's when I began to write."

Edge

"WHAT HAPPENED TO THE BOOK?"

"I gave it away." my voice had reservations in it.

"To a girl?" it was a comment that sounded like a question, but it was rhetorical.

I thought about the answer as her image came to mind, "What makes you say that?"

"Common, typical. People tend to give away or abandon their beliefs for some other surrogate, usually it manifests as some form of love that begets a pseudo-relationship, which in turn fosters resentment to the other for their loss of identity, even though it is they who chose it and turned their back on it to the other person."

"I gave her the book because it was special to me. She knew it was special and I thought she could use it as I did. I believe there is an inherent responsibility in knowledge that should be passed on once its gained. Isn't that the way of things?"

"Depends."

"On?"

"On who you are versus who you choose to be."

"I choose to be responsible and pass on truth though I must accept when it's unwanted." The book slammed and I was encased in darkness again. My thoughts didn't quiet. "We fought a lot. I fight with all my girlfriends."

"Why do you think that is?"

"I think I use some of it as a test and the rest of it because I don't want to become too attached. A friend told me once, "If you want to breakup, get onto a fight and get them to breakup with you, it removes the guilt, but I realize now that it is really some strange perpetuation of my reality, proving to myself that I am not good enough to be with."

"So you can have a reason to breakup?"

"I am a hard person to be with anyway. I have distinct, sometimes unique beliefs and opinions. I figure a woman must have opinions of her own and be able to deal with me, hold her ground and share and not let me break her down in discussions.

If they can't hang, I was right."

"Which was she?"

"Neither, she was neurotic. It was the first time I didn't cause or bring about arguments in the common sense. I stood my ground and allowed her a voice and did what I could to stymie my reactionary side, but that only seemed to fuel her fire. We were both preachy. She was a beautiful person, but she existed deep inside her head. She was constantly absorbed, beyond emotional and very reactionary. Eventually it got to be too much."

"You cared for each other."

"Oh sure, yeah, and there was deep passion like "the War of the Rose's," I think we would have eventually killed each other if it hadn't ended. We had a strange friendship afterwards that lasted just long enough to consider getting back together, but we couldn't even get along in the short term. I woke up one day, had lunch and washed my hands with the hope she would one day grow into a higher truth."

"Did she?"

"You know, it still hurts a little. No she didn't and our last words were furious for other reasons."

"Anger can be remedied and change."

"True, but hurt can last like cancer."

"There is still love there."

"Epics have been written about it… lets change the subject. Perhaps some other day… I will."

"So you passed the book on to her?"

"I realized long ago you can only pass knowledge on, or show people paths. You can't be bound to whether or not someone follows the advice in anyway, because it holds you back from who you are, your truth and where you are going. My intention now is to leave a path of breadcrumbs that people can follow to places I have been, where they may find some sort of truth for themselves. They may find their own path, but anything is better than staying stymied."

Faces from my past relationships smiled at me sweet and sour as I stared ahead through the glass until I suddenly realized I was back. The regulars were still staring at me, all except Twill who was nowhere to be seen.

Inside, the concert was still going on. The girl in the red shoes was at the top of her game, her friends were dancing in their seats and all eyes except the regulars were on her. Outside, the four tables were still occupied, the two girls were still there, but the other two tables had changed faces. Three guys were sitting at the table where the two kids had been and a man was now sitting where the couple had started out.

Back from the darkness I felt myself relax as people came and went. I sat alone inside my head picking at something that was picking at me. A mental scab I was not going to let heal. Or was I the wound? My mind returned...*a little boy...living near a forest with his mother. Playing every day in the trees with the animals.* This thing is turning into more of a children's story by the minute. *One day he saw an old man...* Twill? *trying to climb a mountain.* Twill?

I always considered myself on some sort of journey. There have just been too many "coincidences" that have lead me to places, some obscure and unexplained. "The Road Less Traveled" was one of my favorite poems growing up. I was ten when I read it for the first time and it had a resonance I have never been able to release. Long before "the Razors Edge" there were books and stories that spoke of crossing the metaphysical breach that people so often experienced. An entire subculture of stories which claimed to be based on truth and after "the Razors Edge" I realized I was putting together a puzzle of sorts. I learned the ideas I was having and reading about were nothing new and some questions began to answer themselves. If "the Razors Edge" was true, I learned what became of Larry (at least in my mind). One fact seemed to ring to me. The celebrity of a given novel or story, was sometimes directly related to how much truth it held. The more popular the book the less resonance and visa versa, so as a result I had to allow books to come too me on their own rather than looking for best sellers. And they did. Lessons began to find me.

You journeyed.

I heard Twill's voice as if he was standing behind me and simply accepted it. I couldn't see him and if I went with the other thought... It had already been a strange and illuminating night thus far, but my head was telling me that he was not behind me, rather in my head... Once again I accepted and continued with my ramblings.

"I journeyed yes," I said out loud to the air. "But the frustrating thing was I couldn't share any of what I was learning or discovering with anyone. It was different, off center from accepted norms. It seemed new age, but the people I found who were into the new age were so far into it they had rejected everything outside of it. And that rang true with everyone I found who gained even a little understanding of the riddles. People were absorbed into words that encompassed an identity and the ego told them the thing they found was 'IT', and everyone else was wrong. That idea was unnerving."

And your identity?

"I didn't believe anything should be discounted. I still don't. In fact, I began to believe that everyone, in some respectful sense, was correct. At least they had the right idea, but it seemed that everyone wanted to point fingers at things to make wrong. I felt disconnected as if I had something to tell people that couldn't be readily described. Many friends thought I was crazy."

Were you?

"I began to think so. There are degrees to things as I said before. I turned away from people for a while."

And your identity?

"Well like anything else, it was challenged and twisted by different avenues and venues into things that it wasn't. Many, many people set upon saving my soul."

Your soul? Was that in jeopardy?

"If you ask them it was. Parents, girlfriends, people that knew me and got into conversations… I don't remember how many times I was told I was going to hell for the things that I believe. My only reasoning was that there was some sort of connection between people and their different beliefs that would in turn make everyone equal and able to understand other points of view. One time I was called a communist and that scared me."

Why?

"Because that's when they come to get you, stone you, crucify you for being different… that sounds like I have a god complex."

No it sounds like you have a persecution complex.

"You know for a while I identified myself with gargoyles. Most people see them as evil."

And how did you see them.

"I see them as sort of Yoda-like gurus. I concede the fact that gargoyles are demons, but they are also protectors. In antiquity they were put on the tops of churches as statues and waterspouts to ward off evil."

Gargoyles are demons, ancient and extremely long-lived, watching and learning, the evil-wise ones. They have been given the opportunity to redeem themselves and as a result were placed on the tops of churches as waterspouts for their unique ability to see and identify evil. It is said that their fight to ward off evil and the water constantly rushing through them would eventually cleanse their soul, so that they will be able to step down and move freely among us no longer having to be a waterspout. And since these were the only ones allowed to do so, if you ever see a gargoyle that is not a waterspout, you can be certain it is no longer evil. Its soul has been redeemed. However they will always maintain their horrific features so they will always be reminded of how evil they once were.

How is it you identified yourself with that?

"It was how others viewed me, strange, unworthy, evil to a sense, but most people who spoke to me for any length of time realized who I was. Of course there were always others who tried too "save my soul".

My attention was drawn towards the table with the two girls. One of them was staring at me. The one I wasn't interested in of course and when I turned she quickly looked away. She leaned across to her friend and said something. They leaned in closer to whisper for a moment then laughed out loud. They both turned and glanced at me again. Being so far away I obviously couldn't hear their conversation to begin with, so it baffles me why people do this. Is it some sort of drama people wish to perform?

You should go speak to them.

"Should I?"

Absolutely.

"Because?"

Because you're interested.

"That isn't something that ever came naturally to me. Perhaps from the gargoyle image I kept of myself, or because my own self security was at a minimum."

Let me ask you a question.

"You're asking for permission to ask me a question?"

Choose

INDULGE ME. Clear your head. In regards to life… what do you want?

An image flashed into my head for just a moment. One moment, then they began to flip one after another in no particular direction, women, work, cars, money, career, and freedom… I was in all of them in different setting and moments of life, some gratuitous as I pondered the infinite details of wouldn't it be cool if…? I saw a beautiful woman and I imagined love, then several girls and I thought sex, then I saw myself wealthy, powerful… the crowds of celebrity calling my name… I was smiling, laughing in my head and continued to run the gambit of lives, one to another and another and on faces and emotions in situations that…

DON'T THINK ANSWER! Twill screamed in my head so loud I winced. *That first thought was the purest, truest, most real expression of self you can have, but of course we are already too late, you rethought it.*

The question is simple enough and gets posed every so often, but it never seems to get answered. Those four simple words seem to sum up the crux of humanity.

"How does someone answer a question like that without thinking about it?"

You had an answer, that isn't the issue. The issue is your trust, the faith in yourself, the acceptance of your answer the first answer, which you are unable too accept. The very moment when you should not look at the larger picture you do, negating the image that appears right before you. Another question is: What would you do if you knew you would die tomorrow?

My mind dropped and reached out, but Twill didn't even let me begin.

The problem is that the question is so much broader than the answer. Since you must think, you can look at the question in a few ways. The first is to simply accept and go with the first highest feeling you have. And if you don't like the answer, you may have just learned something about yourself.

The second way takes work. Allow yourself to go in or outside and become deeply cathartic, to reach for the truest vision of your answer and allow it to be... whatever it will, selfish, evil, gratuitous, juvenile, lewd, crude, or just plain dumb and you will have your answer. Given the possibility that you also don't like that answer, it doesn't matter because it is yours to fix, change or manipulate in anyway you see fit.

The last is what most people choose to say. It has only one answer though it is a bit if a failure to delve into possibility.

"I want to be happy." I said.

Of course you do, so in that case a better question might be: What would make you happy?

I couldn't think, at least not the way Twill wanted me to. It had been a long and odd evening and it feels strange to say that my existence was starting to seem insignificant with the world and with everything rushing by my face for hours on end and back, traversing what must be 'time' for I had no other explanation. I had heard the girl in the red shoes sing all of her songs several times now. I had interacted with, if not met, almost every person that was in and would be coming through Pantheons tonight.

I thought about friends and relations from my past. What makes people happy, what would make them happy, why they weren't happy now and such? I remember asking a girlfriend once about her mother who was a devout Christian. By devout I mean she praised the Lord often and invoked Jesus more often than that. I was made to feel less by her, because my beliefs weren't in that vain as if I were a corrupting influence on her daughter, who could do no wrong as she hoped and believed her daughter would eventually come around to the "Christian" way of thinking.

I asked her, "If somehow tomorrow, they found absolute irrefutable proof that God didn't exist what would her mother do?" Her reply was that she didn't think her mother would get out of bed the next day. I took that to mean that in her mother's belief, life itself was insignificant. Having children, moving forward, irrevocably being present and affecting the world didn't matter in the least. Not only that, but it seemed she was living her whole life planning for her death.

Needless to say, once again my opinion wasn't very popular.

If you were to accept and act on the first answer that came into your head, the elemental simplicity of the world would be so wonderful as to be terrifying. Imagine it for a moment. Pose the question to yourself and allow the image of that, which would ultimately make you happy and just be… there in that space… in that moment for a while.

The image came to me strong and fundamentally clear, so simple as to be unreal and thereby unacceptable, so I released it to the back of my head. Realization and conscious came forward.

"It is humbling to realize most of us walk in sleep, a constant dreary listlessness that continues on into the everyday. We live by emotions, which we deny, inevitably denying our own truths that bombard our senses on an unending basis. If we accept that hindsight is twenty-twenty then we must also accept that people generally see us in ways we cannot see ourselves. And if that is truth, then why would there be such animosity and denial. Everyone understands the adage that the truth hurts. Of course those truths do not apply to us.

"We allow society to run our lives all the while getting more and more frustrated at the lack of control. We believe society owes us something and are unwilling to try and do for ourselves. Instead of effort we look for things to make us happy. 'Things' is the operative word. Love and happiness as entities, are intangible. It is strange that we look for the intangible among the tangible were the only happiness is contained in a moment of consumption, with nothing true or lasting which comes from the intangible.

"Success for some is measured in money, others in companionship or family, and others in things, and that being the case then why is it that there aren't more of us who are happy? We visualize happiness just over the next horizon, around the next corner, with the next big paycheck, lover, vacation, movie, or thing purchased. Money obviously isn't the key and that can be found by simply asking anyone who has it. Sex isn't either and though most of us already know that, we continue to search because in the moment of copulation who cares. Things? Things shouldn't even be a question because we never seem to have enough.

"Children, is another great urge, to procreate, to bear the unconditional love, to have a family, to do better with that family than was done in our own. Children are rewarding yes, but the key to happiness they are not. In fact the ill planned birth, with someone who we want to believe is the one and take no responsibility for what it is we are bringing into a relationship and going to inevitably pass on to another life, in the end it turns out to be a much greater burden than we ever imagined."

This is a grand theory, but it is just that, theory, I can already see people shaking their heads at this. But this begs another question to be posed. Are you truly happy?

"No."

Of course not and that brings me back to the previous question, but there are some people who will answer and quickly say yes. And in truth some are. There are those that have taken a different path and found a complacency, which makes them quite content. Of course the argument can be made that happiness is a matter of perspective.

Escuela de Athens

"CONDITIONAL HAPPINESS is not true happiness, of course then you can say that love is the same way, and how often do we find unconditional love?"

The ones that kneel, bow and pray in penance have faithfully taken a path and found happiness.

"That isn't true, that *that* more than most things, is conditional. If something good happens then "it was God's will" or God was watching out for me. Whenever something happens that's bad then "the Lord works in mysterious ways", or "God is testing me" or it is the devil. Through that system there is no faith in the self nor does there need to be. If a person does bad then they are evil, if good they are with God. People forget that levels of good and evil are also perceptions. What one says is bad or evil is not the same as what another might believe. Look at history. So many of the heinous evils have been made by people who justify the things they do, regardless of what the world sees, by a sick mind or their interpretation of what exactly is right and wrong.

"Most people fear what they can't comprehend or understand. Why do people in different cultures do the things they do, for example and in that the basis for all fear is ignorance. Education is freedom from all fear and lack of understanding."

So then explain it, in your understanding.

"God wants everyone to be happy and to do whatever it is

to make themselves happy. Of course it doesn't mean harming others or affecting them in a negative way. But in my interpretation I don't understand the finger pointing the "I'm right your wrong" philosophy of most organizations. There is no respect. Supplication and worship I cannot see."

And what if you're wrong in the end.

"That's the point of belief, faith. How can there be any right or wrong if God loves us all unconditionally? He understands we are human, imperfect and fallible. If we simply do what is best for us by our beliefs and understanding we will be fine, so to speak. You don't give the death penalty to someone who is retarded because they are not clear about what they have done or what has happened to them."

And as for the ones that understand right and wrong and continue to do it?

"There is no perfection. If a mother has a child and that child chooses the wrong path, it does not stop the love from the mother if the love is unconditional. It is still her child, she probably did the best she could and that child did the best it could with what it understood or determined that it needed. In the grandest sense there is no true fault and in the end there will be atonement. The mother may understand that the child may need to be punished however..."

And now we enter the eternal depth of hell.

"No we don't, because hell is supposedly eternal. A mother wouldn't send her son to a place to atone for crimes forever, where they would have no chance of understanding and reclaiming what they have done."

But many religions say that if you don't believe or follow then you will go to hell.

There was an unfamiliar tone to Twill's voice, as if he was smiling though I still couldn't see him. I was frustrated and think it came off.

"Two things seem absolutely ridiculous to me. We are given free will and choice over our lives, but we must make the choices that only follow the just and righteous path. I don't understand how that is freedom of choice. And if you don't follow that path, which by some religions is quite strict and deny the basics of human nature, you will spend eternity in hell, a place so terrible and unforgiving it cannot be comprehended by the human mind.

There is no clearer definition for conditional love.

"All those rules seem sheltered beneath a canopy of fear and fear is not love, it is the opposite. Only a sociopath would make rules like that."

Are you saying Gods is a…

"NO! What I'm saying is fear plays so many roles in our lives today and these things seem to perpetuate it.

"Fear of being alone, in which case we never want to let go, even if we know the situation is wrong for us. We don't take the time to meet someone who will truly compliment us and whom we will compliment. In many cases we have children with the belief, conscious or not, that this is unconditional love. We get very vengeful when we learn that it is not.

"Fear of failure is something easily quelled by not trying because if you don't try you can't fail. That is a valid choice and decision, which is never made, because we don't actually make the decision. We make excuses, reasons not to try. In the end we resent the excuses, blame them for the failure and once again there is anger. Hand in hand is fear of success, which is usually very difficult to see because it's subtle. In most cases it stems directly from childhood when we were told that we won't succeed, or that we don't deserve to succeed. Believing ourselves to be unworthy, we inadvertently sabotage.

"Why do we accept mediocre when we aspire to be higher? 'Good enough isn't.' There are a great many of us that succeed in directions and in careers that have nothing to do with ourselves, rather move towards goals and destinations that our parents set out for us. Both consciously and subconsciously, for better and for worse, a path that may not lead to personal happiness.

"We need to open up, not to others but to ourselves. Some of the most intelligent and insightful people in the world do things for reasons completely unknown to them. Don't be afraid to ask questions because 'Why?' is the most important one of them all. And ask it to yourself first then to others. You will defiantly be surprised at what you might learn."

I HAVE NO INTEREST IN PATRONIZING, BUT…

"But you will."

God Is . . . and We are God's Children

Well…

"A statement like that is only a provisional release of what a person is going to do."

Not necessarily. So once again, I have no interest in patronizing, nor admonishing or being glib, in fact I believe I understand and accept what your are saying. So, if you will allow me a moment?

"Certainly."

Thank you.

Love, by reason of its passion, destroys the in-between which relates us to and separates us from others. (Hannah Arendt)

Love is life. All, everything that I understand, I understand only because I love. Everything is, everything exists, only because I love. (Leo Tolstoy)

Love gives naught but itself and takes naught but from itself.
Love possesses not nor would it be possessed;
For love is sufficient unto love. (Kahlil Gibran)

Love is the extra effort we make in our dealings with those whom we do not like and once you understand that, you understand all. (Quentin Crisp)

Unconditional love is loving your kids for who they are, not for what they do.... I don't mean that we like or accept inappropriate behavior, but with unconditional love we love the children even at those times when we dislike their behavior. (Stephanie

Martson)

Love your enemies. I saw this admonition now as simple, sensible advice. I knew I could face an angry, murderous mob without even the beginning of fear if I could love them. Like a flame, love consumes fear, and thus makes true defeat impossible. (Sarah Patton Boyle)

Conditional love is love that is turned off and on.... Some parents only show their love after a child has done something that pleases them. "I love you, honey, for cleaning your room!" Children who think they need to earn love become people pleasers, or perfectionists. Those who are raised on conditional love never really feel loved. (Louise Hart)

Love means never having to say you're sorry. (Erich Segal)

Love bade me welcome: yet my soul drew back,
Guilty of dust and sin.
But quick-eyed Love, observing me grow slack
From my first entrance in,
Drew nearer to me, sweetly questioning,
If I lacked any thing. (George Herbert)

Love is feared: it dissolves society, it's unpopular, and it's very rare. (Christina Stead)

Love is blind, and greed insatiable. (Chinese proverb)

Love is the reason you were born. (Dorothy Fields)

When love speaks, the voice of all the gods make heaven drowsy with the harmony. (William Shakespeare)

In love's deep womb our fears are held;
there God's rich tears are sown
and bring to birth, in hope new-born,
the strength to journey on. (Rob Johns)

Love conquers everything [Amor vincit omnia]: let us, too, yield to love. (Virgil)

Love requited is a short circuit. (Samuel Beckett)

Love is the direct opposite of hate. (Judith Rossner)

Love is form, and cannot be without important substance. (Charles Olson)

Love is an act of endless forgiveness, a tender look which becomes a habit. (Peter Ustinov)

Pursue love... (New Testament, 1 Corinthians 14:1)

A love that dies has never lived. (Franz Grillparzer)

Love loves no delay; (Thomas Campion)

We love the things we love for what they are. (Robert Frost)

Love will draw an elephant through a key-hole. (Samuel Richardson)
Love is the cheapest of religions. (Cesare Pavese)
Love, I find is like singing. Everybody can do enough to satisfy themselves, though it may not impress the neighbors as being very much. (Zora Neale Hurston)

Love casts the mighty from their thrones,
promotes the insecure,
leaves hungry spirits satisfied,
the rich seem suddenly poor. (Miriam Therese Winter)

Love has its own instinct, finding the way to the heart, as the feeblest insect finds the way to its flower, with a will which nothing can dismay nor turn aside. (Honoré De Balzac)

Love cures people, the ones who receive love and the ones who give it, too. (Karl A Menninger)

While love ceaselessly strives toward that which lies at the hidden most center, hatred only perceives the topmost surface and perceives it so exclusively that the devil of hatred, despite all his terror-inspiring cruelty, never is entirely free of ridicule and of a somewhat dilettantish aspect. One who hates is a man holding a magnifying-glass, and when he hates someone, he knows precisely that person's surface, from the soles of his feet all the way up to each hair on the hated head. Were one merely to seek information, one should inquire of the man who hates, but if one wishes to know what truly is, one better ask the one who loves. (Hermann Broch)

Real love is a pilgrimage. It happens when there is no strategy, but it is very rare because most people are strategists. (Anita Brookner)

Yet love enters my blood like an I.V., dripping in its little white moments. (Anne Sexton)

To love human beings in so far as they are nothing. That is to love them as God does. (Simone Weil)

Love is the source of language, and also its destroyer. (Isabel G MacCaffrey)

"God is Love," we are taught as children to believe. But when we first begin to get some inkling of how He loves us, we are repelled; it seems so cold, indeed, not love at all as we understand the word. (W.H. Auden)

Belief and love, – a believing love will relieve us of a vast load of care. O my brothers, God exists. There is a soul at the center of nature, and over the will of every man, so that none of us can wrong the universe. (Ralph Waldo Emerson)

Falling in love consists merely in uncorking the imagination and bottling the common sense. (Helen Rowland)

There is love of course. And then there's life, its enemy. (Jean Anouilh)

Bitterness imprisons life; love releases it. Bitterness paralyzes life; love empowers it. Bitterness sours life; love sweetens it.

Bitterness sickens life; love heals it. Bitterness blinds life; love anoints its eyes. (Harry Emerson Fosdick)

Yet to sing love, love must first shatter us. (Hilda Doolittle)

The opposite of love is not to hate but to separate. If love and hate have something in common it is because, in both cases, their energy is that of bringing and holding together – the lover with the loved, the one who hates with the hated. Both passions are tested by separation. (John Berger)

The fate of love is that it always seems too little or too much. (Amelia E. Barr)

The opposite of love is not hate, it's indifference. The opposite of art is not ugliness, it's indifference. The opposite of faith is not heresy, it's indifference. And the opposite of life is not death, it's indifference. (Elie Wiesel)

When we lose love, we lose also our identification with the universe and with eternal values – an identification which alone makes it possible for us to lay our lives on the altar for what we believe. (Sarah Patton Boyle)

The moment we choose to love we begin to move against domination, against oppression. The moment we choose to love we begin to move towards freedom, to act in ways that liberate ourselves and others. That action is the testimony of love as the practice of freedom. (Bell Hooks)

The opposite of love is not hate, as many believe, but rather indifference. Nothing communicates disinterest more clearly than distancing. A child cannot feel valued by parents who are forever absorbed in their own affairs. (Dorothy Corkville Briggs)

DePrivy

"Very nice. Profound. Wonderful in and of itself. Many of those quotes seem to concur with what I said and there are many others, but there are some common ones you forgot "Love is s many splendored thing. Love lifts us up where we belong. All you need is love."

And who said all that?

"Well it's a mishmash of quotes from songs, but the entire sentiment is from Moulin Rouge."

It perfectly illustrates the idea. Though in reference to your religious connotations exchange the word God for Love in many of those quotes I mentioned and see what I mean…

…"Yes, now that is exactly my point. Of course spiritual love is not what people usually associate with the word. Romantic love is the more popular brand."

Though there is no difference. Namaste.

"Namasde?"

Namaste. The only reason people see the differences in love is by a given point of view, but the truth is there is no difference if it is given purely and not wanton in anyway. Namaste.

"What is that?"

An east Indian greeting which put simply means 'the God or spirit in me greets, meets, or recognizes, the God or spirit in you.' The greeting acknowledges the equality of all and gives honor to everyone's sacredness. So when one speaks of Love… true love. That should be what they are speaking of. You never answered your own statement.

"What was that?"

The one you fell in love with, just a little bit.

"Not important really." I looked across the way at the girls talking and suddenly felt the urge to leave.

Abandoning temptation doesn't mean it will go away.

"Temptation? The one I am interested in isn't even looking at me, how is that temptation?"

The temptation is for you to make an attempt, to remove the opportunity doesn't address the situation or the fear, which holds you to the belief that you are a gargoyle. Even though you know you are not a gargoyle, there is an inherent fear of the conversation that they will see what's happening in you, what you believe you truly are, and as a result they will shut you down.

Twill's words, right or wrong were upsetting me. I wanted to bolt. Leave the coffee shop, find my car and end the evening now. In another life I would be having a panic attack.

The meaningless words you were told for so long is your belief. Unfortunately the knowledge that your belief is unfounded is meaningless to your core self.

"I have to pee."

You have to reprogram yourself.

"Yeah that will be easy." Through the glass the manager and the old woman were looking at me. I looked at the English guy by the window. He remained stoic and still reading. Drover looked like he was talking to the wall of the hair salon. Fuck it. I rose.

At a boy.

I glanced at the two girls as I passed them and entered Pantheons headed towards the restroom.

Pussy!

I ignored Twill. Perhaps they will be gone when I return.

Quiet time. I find that the older I get more and more I find sanctuary in the bathroom. I can't readily explain this other than it seems the only place free of all responsibility to yourself or others. Sit back, relax and hopefully take all the time you need. There is defiantly a Zen like perfection to the release. Your thoughts are free for those minutes to roam and wander as all you are holding is being purged. Believe it or not I have favorites. Bathrooms should be cool and relaxing with the hum of the air conditioner going, large and silent. The restrooms in airports, some of the more fancy hotel lobbies or convention halls in the middle of the night are usually perfect. Large, sometimes a little posh, the sound of the air conditioner creates an 'Ohm' that echoes as you release. When the room is large with only you for those moments, there is perfection.

The bathroom of Pantheons was small and tried to be hip and fancy at the same time, but the graffiti took care of that. *It smells like roses / Eat it then mouther fuker.* If I don't know how to spell a word I wouldn't write it on a wall, but that's me. *Bouncer*

R.I.P. That one was different and a little curious, I wondered about it. I couldn't stay in here very long. It was a coffee shop, one bathroom and co-ed at that. I just really needed to pee and get some air from Twill. Where was Twill anyway? He wasn't in my head after I walked away from the table and I am certain he could be if he was so inclined.

I flushed and thoroughly washed my hands, taking as much time as possible. Maybe I'll just go get may car and go home. I checked my watch as I dried my hands. It was only ten thirty. Right now a couple seated against the far wall would be in the middle of an argument and nearby heads would turn. The argument would be started because the boyfriend would be apparently enraptured at a song the girl in the red shoes was playing and make a comment about it. I've seen the argument several times tonight, but once it didn't happen because I was at their table talking to them.

The night swam in my head and my thoughts drifted again on where I was and what exactly was happening to me.

Someone tried the handle. It was the guy. He needed a break from the argument with his girlfriend.

I finished up, grabbed the key, opened the door and held it up as I passed by him.

"Hey thanks," he said sounding exasperated.

"Sure Andy," Oops, that was a slip up.

"Hey? Do I know you?" he asked staring at me.

"Uh…no, uh…when you ordered."

"Oh. Cool thanks," he took the key.

"Sure thing." I walked away and glanced around the room wanting to avoid the outside for a moment more. My attention was drawn to the girlfriend. She was pretty steamed and staring angrily at the girl in the red shoes.

Intimate

SOMETHING IN ME was drawn forward again. He would be in there for a few minutes, but somehow I don't think it mattered. I stared at his girlfriend, staring at the girl in the red shoes and then I was moving towards her, feeling the moment seize before I… "Hello

Arlene." I sat down in the boyfriend's chair.

She was as shocked as I was. "What? Do I know you?"

"No."

"My boyfriend is sitting there."

"I know it's fine he will be a little while. How are you?"

"Fine." She was annoyed at me, but I made no advance.

I turned to look at the girl in the red shoes.

"Do you want something?" she asked. She was really pissed.

"She is good isn't she?"

"Yeah! Too good," her attention was drawn towards the stage. "Bitch!" I heard her whisper.

"Now do we have to be like that?"

"Like what?"

"Such language and energy to a person you don't even know?"

"I didn't say anything."

I was stumped for a moment, but recovered quickly. "What's wrong?" I said the words aloud though I was not speaking directly to her. Rather I imagined I was speaking to the sum of her being. I felt them reach and penetrate.

She felt it as well. Somehow I could see it evident on her face, but I wasn't facing her. "That girl and my fucking boyfriend..." she trailed off.

"Is something going on between them?"

"You know how guys are. I saw something, a look and he specifically wanted to come here tonight."

"So something is going on?"

The answer was obvious, but she was upset and trying to deny it. "He wants her. That last song she played. She even looked at him and smiled."

"So?"

The girl sat there seething, not answering.

The girl in the red shoes nodded and smiled to friends and members of the audience that were enjoying themselves. I deliberately turned my head and gave a slight nod towards each person as she did so. And I know Arlene saw it as well.

"Umm..." I felt her energy soften. "Why do guys do that?" she finally said.

"What exactly do guys do?"

She did not speak. *They always do this and they do it to me.* I heard the whisper again.

"What is so bad about you?"

She turned to me. I kept my eyes on the concert. "Nothing."

"Really?"

She was pouting now. I imagined her opening up not to me or to her boyfriend, but to herself. Allowing a level of realization deeper than the situation itself. She didn't speak, but I felt her soften. I looked where I had been standing and saw myself, and suddenly I was staring across the room at Arlene again, seated alone waiting for her boyfriend. The girl in the red shoes started playing the song she had been playing a moment ago and I continued to the front door.

A hand touched my forearm. Just simply touched it and I was seized by the contact. I looked down to see the old woman smiling at me. She nodded a greeting. "Rasha." I said nodding back. The woman put her hands together in prayer and gave me a nod. I felt light.

The restroom door opened. Andy stepped out, gave the key to Noaisha and went back to his seat. He was exasperated. Their conversation continued, but it looked as if the tone was different. He moved his seat around to sit beside her. They hugged and kissed, and continued watching the concert.

@ The Met

OUTSIDE I WENT STRAIGHT back to my table that now had four chairs around it. Twill was seated back in his, mine was vacant and the other two were apparently taken from the table where the girls had been sitting, because the two girls were seated in them. Both of them smiled at me as I sat.

"Ah, I was worried you got lost." Twill graciously opened. "We were just discussing the sociological view of relationships between men and women today as opposed to those in the past."

I shot Twill an eye. I'm certain he felt it, but of course he smiled and continued.

"This is Evelyn and Sandra, they work at the hair salon next door."

"Really?" I tried to sound enthusiastic and nodded to both

girls. "Returning to the scene of the crime." They both laughed. I gave them both a quick once over now that I had them up close. I couldn't remember which one I was interested in now they were both looking at me. The situation had me confused moreover because for some reason they were both intensely familiar to me. "And what is the current consensus at this point?"

"Well we seem a bit divided. Evelyn has adopted what in my terms, is a cynical, somewhat atheistic point of view of the world today."

Evelyn was much shorter than Sandra who was a little taller than myself and she sat shaking her head as Twill gave his description. "No I was saying that people need to take responsibility for the decisions they make and not blame anyone else, like society, their situation, some other person, or God for the seemingly unfortunate crap that happens."

"Well put..." Twill replied. "And Sandra has retained a great deal of her faith in humanity and society which allows for magic to still remain a tangible possibility."

Sandra nodded and smiled.

"And...?" Twill turned to me.

"Oh no," I said. "I would not dare impose myself. I would much rather hear your opinion."

Both girls turned to Twill who smiled at me broadly. "My opinion doesn't matter."

The girls turned to me and nodded.

"How can your opinion not matter?"

"In this context, my opinion has no real frame of reference as I am an individual who is in the wintered twilight of his years. I am speaking to individuals who are still youthful, walking in the shadow of beginnings. No, this question is for you my lad and not for an old man's remembrance of decades before you were a zygote."

The girls kept staring at me. I was deflated by Twill not having to entertain any sort of opinion. "I..." I let my thoughts begin their natural twist shifting into numerous possibilities. "I would say that I agree with both of your opinions." I replied.

"Um..." Twill coughed. "I must call foul on that answer." The girls laughed and I hoped I didn't blush, if I did it was dark and they might not notice it.

"Do you remember last Christmas?" I threw Twill a challenging look, but the question was generalized and rhetorical.

Both girls nodded as the corners of Twill's mouth turned up slightly.

"And how about the Christmas before that?"

The girls nodded again.

"Now how many months ago was that?" I started to address the table, continuing before anyone could answer. "But as you think about that, think about the fact that the average person is on earth, for only one thousand months. And if you sleep every night or… almost every night," I dropped my voice and winked. The girls smiled knowingly. "And if you have a job, over half of that time is taken away. That leaves us all with about five hundred months to carve out all the experiences life has to offer."

The girls were both smiling.

"If you think about a minute. Sixty seconds is a short almost insignificant unit of time for some. The New York minute is a metaphor for a moment, singular and infinite, where everything in the world can suddenly change for the better or worse. And these days it's a fact, where simply crossing the street could put you face to face with a bullet, a car, or a bomb. Of course, it can also put you face to face with that person you've been looking for your entire life. I believe that there is a reason for everything and coincidence is something we say just to mask our fear of the unknown. I think we should face and embrace our fears. It is the only true path to absolute freedom."

Twill continued to smile and threw me a wink.

"So just for one minute, accept what, accept where and who we are. With all of our imperfections seen or unseen, real or imagined, we are all absolute perfect beings. Of course we are also completely, totally and utterly mortal and will eventually die, here, on this planet. This big blue unpredictable marble of people, germs and machines each of us must navigate every minute of everyday. And by that, every minute should count and not be taken as some trivial punch line that passes on and on to the next. Nothing is trivial."

Everyone was held and Twill nodded to me as I continued.

"You know I just realized, if there are six billion people on earth and we all want to find that right person who is one on a million. Then that must mean each of us has six thousand Mr. or Mrs. Rights', right?"

The girls were smiling, Twill nodded.

"But just for one minute, accept the possibility that this is it. And when it's over BLACK... nothing. It could cause you to make some different decisions in your life. Living for the minute, doesn't mean living life on the edge, without any regard for the feelings or safety of others. Rather it means living for yourself and not worrying about what others might think say or believe, because when you get right down to it we are all born to live and then to die again and there is no life except what we make. Time moves on while life is something that happens while we sit making plans, whether or not we decide to participate. If you accept God or not when your time is up, it is up and you never can tell when that might be."

I looked at Twill and each of the girls for a moment.

"I believe? I believe that there are infinite possibilities in each minute and we should not hesitate to suck the life, out of life, in every single minute. So as I said I agree with both of you, only a little differently."

"Wow." Sandra said.

Vexed

EVELYN WAS SMILING, but I could see she had not heard the words. Her eyes were chewing on me, inch my minute, devouring me through her imagination. I realized now which was which. I did not want Evelyn and as fortune would have it Sandra was now looking at me.

Twill didn't speak he only nodded at me, smiling beneath his beard.

"Well that closes it I guess." Sandra said.

Evelyn broke eye contact with me to look around the table, "Not really, it's too positive. It doesn't reflect reality."

"Doesn't it?" I asked.

"No. It's your opinion and that's all."

"My point of view?"

"Exactly, just because your opinion agrees and includes both of ours it doesn't mean it's gospel."

"Evelyn!" Sandra said.

I raised my hand slightly towards Sandra, "Your saying it's

my opinion?"

"Yes." Evelyn was a challenger for apparently no reason.

"But aren't all things? Doesn't everything depend on an individuals point of view, a smattering of personal right and wrong with nothing to be taken as gospel?"

Evelyn balked for a second and I realized the look on her face must have been similar to mine when Twill sat down.

"If one was to consider the definition of good and bad, consider evil. What is evil?" I asked looking around the table.

"Killing someone." Sandra said.

"Just killing?"

Evelyn didn't answer, but I could see her planning an attack.

"The word evil brings many images to mind. All real and viable of course… all in your opinion. However what you consider bad, wrong or evil could be common practice to another. By that rational, if people didn't do the things you thought were wrong, how would you know you were right without putting things into context?"

"I would know." Evelyn replied.

"Really? You would understand the horrors of genocide if you hadn't seen a few thousand people murdered for no reason, but would you really understand its level and impact, where it could lead if we didn't have the holocaust? Probably not. That knowledge, the signs of how it arrived and became what it did, we would do well to understand so that something similar never happens again."

Evelyn was ready to speak, but sat back deflated.

Sandra was smiling and looking at her friend.

Twill looked asleep.

There was an awkward silence that lasted several moments and I figured Evelyn was about done with me, and ready to go. "You both work next door? Hairdressers?"

"Stylists." Sandra corrected.

"You like it?"

"It's okay, it has its ups and downs."

"Like?"

"Well the money is good and if you have large clientele you can get good tips."

"No reporting?"

She shook her head. "Well, you report a little to make it look better, but some don't report at all. Our place isn't corporate so its okay to make your own hours, take days off when you want. There is a lot of freedom in it."

"All positive."

"Well it does get busy and by busy I mean busy. You can get stacked up ten clients deep on some days."

"You can." Evelyn said looking at Sandra.

"She hasn't been working too long and doesn't have a large client base yet, but yours is growing." She turned to her friend.

Evelyn rolled her eyes.

"You do get a lot of cuts," Sandra held up her hands the backs of which were scarred. "And some hair can get you like splinters."

"Some?"

"The more course straight hair, Asian hair is thick straight and if they get you just right they can be like little splinters and if you get them under your fingernails… ouch?"

"You don't have a large client base?" I asked Evelyn.

"Not yet, but my regulars are growing, I've only been cutting hair for two years." Evelyn seemed to be calming and getting back into the conversation.

"And you?"

"Oh I've been cutting for over ten years." Sandra said.

"You must like it. You know I find it interesting that the Mohawk has suddenly come back."

"That's true." Sandra agreed.

"And that it has found a place in relatively civilized society. Not the grandiose, foot long spikes of the punk era, with different colors flagging themselves around town." I waved my hand above my head.

"No they're shorter, neatly cropped spikes about an inch or two high."

"Yes, around a full head of hair as a style, and the wearers are not the angry leather clad "delinquents" usually associated with them, but people apart of the general working week. Brush it down and they would look alright in a business suit as they head off to work."

"I have a few clients like that. Thirty something 'punks'."

Sandra said.

"Is that what you call them?"

"Well it works, they don't mind it. Some people have to sort of disguise their home lives these days."

"Well yes. I doubt the Mohawk will find a place in the average board meeting for some decades to come."

"This is true." Sandra was getting quite comfortable, while tension was vibrating off Evelyn again.

"You know they say hair dressers are like bartenders."

"What?" The challenge was in Evelyn's voice. She seemed to be just itching for an argument, but couldn't begin without any provocation.

"That's true. You know Eve'. It's advice and stories. All the time! Sometimes it gets a little boring or overwhelming, that's when you finish them fast and call the next client. All day there are different opinions…" She emphasized the word. "Jokes, gossip, advice moving through twenty to seventy people in a given day. There are no secrets, not really."

Evelyn was pouting with her body and looked hard at Sandra, ready to leave.

Sandra ignored her. "What do you do?"

Twill was still asleep.

"I…" no words came. No pictures were in my head. "I…work…I am a traveling minstrel." Why the hell did I say that? I saw Twill's beard twitch around his mouth.

Sandra laughed. "Really?"

"No, I'm a writer… sort of."

"What do you write?"

"Well nothing at the moment I'm trying to get something going. I've been blocked for a while."

"So it's basically a hobby." Evelyn said.

Sandra felt the slap and released a sigh of frustration.

It was my turn to be deflated, "If that's your opinion, then you are absolutely correct."

Evelyn was done with me. "We need to go." She said to Sandra. They rose together, but Evelyn was faster.

Sandra stood, her hand coming out of her purse as she did so. She leaned over and placed her card on the table in front of me. If you need a cut… or want to talk or…" Her voice trailed off.

It was now Evelyn's turn to sigh as she walked away.

"Thank you I will. I shook her hand."

She turned to Twill who still looked asleep. She whispered, "Nice meeting you 'two-il'."

The last word was mumbled and faded, but I thought… What did she say? She walked away to catch up with Evelyn who was already past Drover. Did she just call him by his name or did I hear something else?

"Nice girls." Twill said.

"What did she just call you?"

"Did she call me something?"

"I thought she did."

"Oh, what do you think she called me?"

"I thought…" Twill had an amused look on his face again. "Forget it."

. . . Eve'

"WHAT WAS THE POINT OF THAT? Why did you bring them over here like that?"

"That wasn't what you wanted?" Twill was nonchalant.

"That isn't the point."

"So you didn't want to meet the girl you were looking at? You didn't want to talk, get her number?"

I didn't have a reply. Ideally it is always a thought when you stare at someone across the room that fate or a friend would intervene and you get to meet them. I had nothing to complain about. I just didn't like being out of control.

"Then it…?"

"NO!" I cut Twill off fast from the question that would almost certainly be a response to my thoughts. The frustration was almost overwhelming. I stared though the glass brooding, thinking of the girl that just gave me her number. I looked over at the salon. Drover was still sitting on the brick flower box and as I looked he turned towards me. His teeth fell out of lips in an inhuman grin that kept expanding until it was painfully frightening. I zoomed in the face that seemed to growl at me, a black Cheshire cat with an Afro. I was transfixed and frightened at the same time and suddenly his mouth opened and I was yanked forward into those homeless teeth and I was gone.

"I need a hair cut." I heard myself say, staring at a glass case, filled top to bottom with product, popular and obscure brand name bottles of hair care, shampoos, conditioners, gels and such.

"Certainly sir it will be about five minutes." I turned to face Sandra standing behind the counter punching something into the register. "Twenty-three dollars." She said to a man standing with his back to me.

"There you go…keep it."

Sandra took the twenty and the ten. "Thank you."

The man turned to face me, Twill stopped and smiled. "They do a great job here." I looked up at the rat's nest perched atop Twill's head as he gave me a wink and walked out the door. Outside was dark and Sandra moved past me, locked the door and pulled a string hanging from the fluorescent open sign and the light went out.

"Oh, are you closed?" I asked.

"We are now, you're the last one."

"Well I don't want to hold you up."

"No, it's no problem." She moved to her chair, brushed it off and unfolded a fresh apron. "Have a seat."

I sat down. She draped the apron over me and turned the chair around to face the mirror. I stared at my reflection, awkward, a strange bewildered look in my eyes. "I'm bald." I said aloud.

"Uh huh." Sandra said as if the fact didn't matter in the slightest. "So how do you want it?"

"Oh, just…" I wasn't sure what to say. "I trust you." The words came out with nothing else in my head.

She nodded and set the clippers up. There were two other stylists and one other client had just been let out. At the far end Evelyn was cleaning up her station, sweeping hair and wiping down the glass. "Do the cleaners come tonight or tomorrow?"

"Tomorrow." Sandra said she was going through drawers one by one looking for something.

"Damn that means we have to clean tonight?"

"Yes it does." She pulled out a small tube and squeezed something in to her hand. "You shave your head?"

"Yes." Why did she ask?

"Most people think that when they shave, they cut all the hair, but did you know there could be as much as an inch of hair hidden beneath the scalp?"

"Really?" I touched my scalp, skin, muscle and skull. I wondered where I was hiding an inch. Whenever I got an ingrown hair it showed up as a grotesque welt that would hurt and annoy until it came to a head or I was able to pull it out. I have pilled inch long hairs out before. The skin boil was huge.

"This might tingle a little." She said.

"You mean burn?"

"Well… guys are babies, so it might burn a little." She started rubbing a chemical into my scalp, messaging it in. Her hands were excellent and my head lulled as she manipulated it. My eyes rolled, then my forehead began to glisten with sweat. "Give that a minute." I heard the sizzle coming from the top of my head as the heat welled.

Sandra began to clean.

"I have got to go on a diet." The other stylist said aloud.

"What, what are you talking about?" Sandra said.

"I'm serious, my butt is getting huge."

Evelyn looked at her. "Come on now, you look fine."

"You know I can see it, but I feel…you ever get that, you know. Not bloating, but my clothes aren't fitting right, at least not like they usually do."

"You know I'm not as bad as I used to be, Sandra you remember." Evelyn started modeling herself in the mirror. "I would go crazy of I went past one hundred and nine, but I will say that over the last year I have become more comfortable and accepting my weight and size, since I started working with that trainer."

"You mean working that trainer!" Sandra chimed in and they all laughed.

"That's true, but I was able to realize what is healthy and what is pretty."

"You know I don't know any girl that considers herself pretty, I mean logically pretty. Some are full of themselves, but the average girl, including us, we don't know how pretty we are, like Jessica. Jessica is a large woman, but she is…"

"Curvy."

"Curvy and voluptuous, and you know it works on her. If she lost all the weight like she says she wants to, she wouldn't be as pretty and she might loose all of those curves."

"Well you have curves. I know, but I'm getting older and you know I can see things happening, I mean my mom was the same way. When she was younger she looked just like me, I mean thin up top and like a ghetto booty, but when she got forty… I mean she still has it and she kept the curves, but she just kind of…"

"Swelled."

"Exactly."

"But you're not, I mean you're fine."

"I'm okay, but you know I'm always aware you know. I asked my daughter and you know what she said. ""Well you know you are getting fatter mom.""

"No she didn't."

"Yeah, well, I had to get it out of her, she didn't want to answer."

"Is she skinny."

"Oh yeah, like a rail and she's already taller than me. She takes after her dad."

"Well I don't need to loose weight I just need a little…little little…" Evelyn said. The girls laughed.

My head had ceased to tingle and it felt like layers of my skin were starting to burn off. In the mirror my head had turned black in the first ten seconds and now I could see wisps as I turned from side to side. I wanted to say something, but the "men are babies" comment had me keeping my mouth shut. Sweat was pouring off my forehead now and I kept wiping it with my hand from under the apron. As the cleaning and conversation drew on, it felt as if they had forgotten all about me and I decided not to interrupt the intimate details that I was privy as a fly on the wall.

"What about your trainer?"

"He has a girlfriend so when we do, it's fast and rare."

"What do you have at home?" Sandra's tone was implying but she said no more.

"Oh I have something, but I don't like it, plastic and hummin' up in me. I don't like working it like that, I don't even like condoms."

"You're doing it wrong girl. You don't need it on. You just need IT. Jut something in there, you know, to fill the space. That space needs to be filled and then you can do whatever you need. I have never even put batteries in mine."

"I want to get one of those machines."

"The little pocket things with the remote? Yeah my husband bought me one of those and he kept the remote. It was good, but it can be too much. I wore it once when we went out. And he wouldn't warn me when he would turn it on. A screamed in the restaurant, because I was shocked. And my problem is I want him so I get so wet that…" She trailed off. " I wouldn't do it again unless I wore a pad I swear."

"No there are other machines. Big machines. You never seen them with a big dildo on the end and they move right up in you while you sit on them?"

"Really?"

"You're nasty." Sandra said turning to me. "Oh my god. I forgot you were there. Oh my god, we need to rinse this come on." She wiped my forehead, which was drenched in sweat again and told me to come with her. I followed her to one of the sinks at the end. Both of the girls avoided my eyes and cleaned vigorously.

"Lay back." Sandra turned the water on and began to rinse my head. It felt cool, but my scalp was throbbing tenderly. I wondered how she was going to shave it. She ran her fingers through the new growth of hair that had suddenly sprung up arrived, but the euphoria was gone.

She pulled a towel down from the shelf and started to dry it. My scalp hurt, bad. I gritted my teeth.

"Okay." She leaned me up from the laidback position and I followed her to the chair.

"It defiantly tingled."

"Yes, but not that bad right?"

I didn't answer.

Fallen

IN THE MIRROR I had hair. Stringy immature wisps had sprouted all over my scalp, thin and underdeveloped. I thought of a Chia Pet. I ran my fingers through it as Sandra turned on the clippers. It still hurt, bad. She moved behind me and I felt the cold machine touch my right temple and began to slide up. I winced and waited imagining that more than hair would be removed in this instance, remembering a friend who described the aftermath of a third degree burn on his arm.

He tweezers snipped, missed, snipped again and clenched to remove the crinkles that resemble black toilet paper strips, from my overcooked sausage. He told me he screamed through the towel he used to bite down on as his muscles pulled against the restraints. Misery measured in quarter inches. His charred screams release to reveal pink, newborn flesh unburned.

The clipper moved over my head and dropped hair onto my shoulder. I waited for something to catch as she cut everything off. Her face was the picture of anguish. The entire scalp was tender and beneath the hair, red as a bad sunburn.

"Oh, I left it on too long."

She was careful then, moving around to the front and side, which was always the most delightful thing about getting a haircut from a beautiful woman. There was no helping the breasts getting right in your face.

She winced as she cut." Does it hurt?"

"A bit."

"I'm so sorry."

My head looked like it had been smeared in iodine. A great red birthmark covered my entire scalp. From behind me I heard a gasp and could see Evelyn and the other girl staring at me in the mirror.

"Ever had this happen guys?" Sandra asked.

"Not that bad, is he allergic?"

"No, I don't think so, I left it on too long."

"Maybe some lotion?"

Sandra looked worried, but for some reason I wasn't, more amused than anything. I felt heat radiating off my head and my brow was still sweating.

"I am so sorry."

"It's okay, really. I don't think it will kill me so…" There really wasn't anything to say. Evelyn came over with some type of skin moisturizer with aloe and Sandra pulled a generous amount and began to gently rub it allover my head.

"How does that feel?"

"Nice."

"Perhaps we'll let that sit for a minute."

"Do you have a towel?" I motioned to my forehead.

Sandra gave me a towel and I wiped my forehead through the apron. She started cleaning again, but the salon was silent now. The girls were just about done and the situation had become uncomfortable.

I waited, staring into the mirror and once again they seemed to forget about me. Completely. The conversation turned to common banter. The other girl left. Sandra finished cleaning, then bagged the register money and receipts. Then as if I didn't exist at all, she and Evelyn went to the back, the lights went off and they both walked out together. I got up and moved to the front door, staring through the glass at them as they locked the door and walked over to Pantheons. They put their stuff down on the table outside and went in to get their drinks.

Drover was seated on the brick flower box right in front me and I could see my table. Twill layback comfortably looking through the glass and seated opposite him I stared at myself. Which meant I wasn't here? Or I wasn't here? Or did this even happen?

"Strange, isn't it?" The voice behind me had a thick British accent.

I turned to a figure sitting in Evelyn's chair near the back. The entire room was cloaked in darkness and I couldn't see the face.

"I understand that this is all hard to fathom, but here you are, and before you ask, I am not here to explain shit to you."

The vibe coming from the figure was cold and unfeeling, and even as my eyes adjusted to the darkness he remained in shadow. "Who are...?"

"No questions from you either I am not that old fart out there."

I moved forward past the counter to Sandra's chair, my head beginning to feel better, but I was still sweating. I wiped my forehead and removed the residual lotion from my scalp. I couldn't tell how bad it was in the dark. I took off the apron and sat back in the chair.

The figure in Evelyn's chair continued. "I don't honestly care what it is you think, want, or do through all of this. I despise the insidiousness of this entire thing." He took a breath slowly. "I want you to tell me of evil."

"Excuse me?"

"Tell me of evil."

"I don't under..." The figure released an exasperated sigh and as he breathed a tremendous heat struck me and I saw priests and bishops in ordained garb torturing in the name of the divine. Cruelty wrought from the understanding of pain. Others letting blood, pulling organs shown to victims with forks impaling their chests, chins, and feet.

A long cruel looking three pronged blade dug into me and was twisted by a masked individual and I had no choice, but to release a most inhuman wrench that deafened my own ears.

"Happy times, medieval and wonderful. The things imagined in those days unmatched now."

I stared at the dark figure in the heat of the salon growing.

"Tell me of evil." He said calmly.

My mind raced into itself, levels of giving and tearing away by pains as others thwarted life in its perceived perfection.

"No! Tell me!"

I released and burrowed beyond myself. I saw mobs killing one, thousands killing each other as others looked on. I saw a world of love and happiness denied by powers that rule. I saw torture and then I saw children…

"Yess."

The salon was becoming a sulfurous stinking furnace and my head began to tingle again. I saw rape, sodomy, I saw lives twisted and released as so much waste. I heard tears and screams and incoherent mutterings from those doing, as well as those receiving. Inhuman was not a word for it, for it was human.

"Yesss." The word came with a sigh of ecstasy.

I descended into the heat allowing it to consume me. There was a foundation here. A base. A cause. The sickness is not without cause. There is a catalyst. As I descended, the heat increased until I felt the blisters begin on my face, my arms, and back. I shut my eyes for fear they might just burst. I tried to breathe and I felt my lungs singe.

"Yessss."

I wasn't stopping. Even as I reached the bottom where there was nothing, but an ashen landscape, my skin now charred and black as midnight glistening in the oils of fat secreting to cook myself in the juice of my self. I was aware of bone moving, crinkling and crispy remains and as a superheated toxic breeze crept over the land that also went and with that, I burst.

"YESSSS!"

All of this and yet I was aware, and through blind nonexistent eyes I moved. This was a rouse. In this place all was remembered. Screams inhuman, animalistic and deafening, and though I had no ears to listen I perceived. This hellish land, so hot nothing could escape it, except that which wasn't, as is the same in life. The spirit remains to accomplish, to move forward to achieve the everlasting.

Through spirit any mountain will move.

Delve

I WENT DEEPER. I HAD TO, further. This terra firma scaped-scene was not the end. It could not be the end in this existence because in this sense I did not exist and I sensed it. All around was flat, a chard volcanic basin scraped from the excrement of souls tortured to their ends. If I could tell the odor, if such a thing could be perceived in the heat of this place, it would conger images of lost abandonment so profound as to bring death instantly after dropping into fetal self-embracement's. Frightful looks of terror would leave all parts of a body lifeless, as if no animation had ever penetrated its smallest cell.

All of this… did not exist.

The images wrought were remembered, compounded from memory gathered and worsened by eternity as to seem inexhaustible.

Ahead was a hole, a great crater in this landscape, a gaping maw that told of such a wretched finality nothing would ever emerge from it.

Even the screams died away as I approached from fear of consumption.

At the precipice I was alone, abandoned in an arena of abandonment, void of body and blood. Though I had heart, I was the sum of my essence and I breathed without lungs in a land of no oxygen. I moved out above the abysm to the center felling a drawing thrust of emptiness. The want held me, but I was not supposed to be here and now that I was, something began to resist.

I was not wanted.

I held myself, waiting for a consuming tug from the orifice and I released.

The descent, if that is what I felt, was with such ferocity that for a moment I was afraid. Around me the wailing began again. Coming, I thought, from those who had gone before me into this place. I began to descend faster through the heat into in the sudden blackness of void.

I perceived nothing. I felt nothing. I knew nothing. I was frozen, cold, but something was here. Above me I saw only the great fall I had passed from. The opening had sealed.

I waited. There was something here.

Faintly I could still hear and feel the fear above me though I was not afraid.

Everything created went up away from me. Everything manufactured in this place went back up the way I had come.

I could see the fear as it came rising, reaching and gathering momentum in its assent.

And somewhere I understood. Somewhere outside and inside at the core of that which was my self, I understood.

I waited for it to germinate.

I was nowhere, but everywhere at once in a foretelling remembrance.

I was.

"What is it you wish?" I asked the dark figure in the corner.

"I am aware of you, your descent into the pit, your angst in doings, your anger, hate. I have watched and seen the frustration charging your soul to act through flashes of malevolence. I know the bowel in you as none can testify. And I am aware of your awareness. I want you to tell me the blackness lying active in your soul. I want you to tell me of evil."

I released myself into the ether that was, from where I found myself, all above and ahead of me. I allowed myself to be stripped to my core nothing and I answered. "Fear is the main source of superstition, and one of the main sources of cruelty. To conquer fear is the beginning of wisdom, in the pursuit of truth as in the endeavor after a worthy manner of life. That is a quote by Bertrand Russell." I exhaled in the heat of the salon and waited.

The dark figure in Evelyn's chair shifted and exhaled again. I felt the breathing heat stroke me in the salon oven. "No." he said calmly. And through gritted teeth the next words were spoken. "I asked you to tell me of evil and you..."

"...and I told you of fear." I interrupted him. The heat was maddening, but my confidence was gaining as my knowledge expanded from the nothing I found myself swimming through.

"Tell me… of evil." He exhaled again and I felt my face singe. I wondered of I had any hair on my face left let alone my head.

I touched something inside myself and Twill's face came to me like a freight train. I saw where my head was going. I smiled in the dark salon, sat back in my chair and crossed my legs mocking the figure silhouetted in black. "I will tell you all I know if you will allow me."

"Certainly."

"Thank you."

Lost

FROM WHERE I FOUND MYSELF, I rose, at speed, absorbing everything I came across beginning with the manufactured warning chirps and terrified screams of the supposed damned, through the grounded heat that turned all things molten and ash, and continued. In the gaining of myself, words began to arrive on their own and in the salon furnace, I began to speak.

Fear always springs from ignorance. (Ralph Waldo Emerson)

Ignorance is learned; innocence is forgotten. (José Bergamín)

Ignorance itself is without a doubt a sin for those who do not wish to understand; for those who, however, cannot understand, it is the punishment of sin. (St. Augustine)

An ignorance of Marx is as frequent among Marxists as an ignorance of Christ is among Catholics. (José Bergamín)

Ignorance is an evil weed, which dictators may cultivate among their dupes, but which no democracy can afford among its citizens. (William, Lord Beveridge)

The ignorance and darkness that is in us, no more hinders nor confines the knowledge that is in others, than the blindness of a mole is an argument against the quick-sightedness of an eagle.

(John Locke)

The ignorance of one voter in a democracy impairs the security of all. (John Fitzgerald Kennedy)

Most ignorance is vincible ignorance. We don't know because we don't want to know. (Aldous Huxley)

The greater the ignorance the greater the dogmatism. (Sir William Osler)

Knowledge will forever govern ignorance: And a people who mean to be their own Governors, must arm themselves with the power which knowledge gives. (James Madison)

Bigotry is the disease of ignorance, of morbid minds; enthusiasm of the free and buoyant. Education and free discussion are the antidotes of both. (Thomas Jefferson)

I say there is no darkness but ignorance. (William Shakespeare)

War is peace. Freedom is slavery. Ignorance is strength. (George Orwell)

Education costs money, but then so does ignorance. (Claus, Sir Moser)

It is certain, in any case, that ignorance, allied with power, is the most ferocious enemy justice can have. (James Baldwin)

Nothing in the world is more dangerous than sincere ignorance and conscientious stupidity. (Martin Luther King, Jr.)

The figure shifted in his seat, the temperature in the salon grew hotter still and my eyes began to squint from pain. Tears, sweat and saliva began to pour out of me as my body attempted to cool itself by any and all means, but I continued.

Absolute power can only be supported by error, ignorance and prejudice. (Philip Dormer Stanhope)

From ignorance our comfort flows. The only wretched are the wise. (To the Hon. Charles Montague)

I count religion but a childish toy,
And hold there is no sin but ignorance. (Christopher Marlowe)

There can be no more ancient and traditional American value than ignorance. English-only speakers brought it with them to this country three centuries ago, and they quickly imposed it on the Africans – who were not allowed to learn to read and write – and on the Native Americans, who were simply not allowed. (Barbara Ehrenreich)

Ideas are only lethal if you suppress and don't discuss them. Ignorance is not bliss, it's stupid. Banning books shows you don't trust your kids to think and you don't trust yourself to be able to talk to them. (Anna Quindlen)

Crimes increase as education, opportunity, and property decrease. Whatever spreads ignorance, poverty and, discontent causes crime.... Criminals have their own responsibility, their own share of guilt, but they are merely the hand.... Whoever interferes with equal rights and equal opportunities is in some ... real degree, responsible for the crimes committed in the community. (Rutherford Birchard Hayes)

It is fortunate that each generation does not comprehend its own ignorance. We are thus enabled to call our ancestors barbarous. (Charles Dudley Warner)
There are two things which cannot be attacked in front: ignorance and narrow-mindedness. They can only be shaken by the simple development of the contrary qualities. They will not bear discussion. (John Emerich Edward Dalberg)

My sight shifted and the salon began to grow dark in my blindness. My eyes no longer felt as if they were streaming tears but I was wondering of they might burst from the heat.

The figure in the seat shifted again, "Stop! This is not what I asked you." he was agitated but I had no intention of stopping, even if my eyes burst from me.

Well I am certainly wiser than this man. It is only too likely that neither of us has any knowledge to boast of; but he thinks that he knows something which he does not know, whereas I am quite conscious of my ignorance. At any rate it seems that I am wiser than he is to this small extent, that I do not think that I know what I do not know. (Socrates)

"You are certainly testing." The figure stood in the knowledge that I knew exactly who and what he was. "I want you to…"

My eyes could see nothing now, there was only heat and sweat and suddenly a thick ooze began running down my pained face. It spilled past my mouth. I had no more tears or use for them, but I would finish. "…I cannot tell a thing without first understanding it and I know what evil is and know where it stems from, lack of knowledge breeds fear and causes evil."

Ignorance is the mother of all evils. (François Rabelais)

Ignorance is not innocence but sin. (Robert Browning)

Ignorance is the curse of God,
Knowledge the wing wherewith we fly to heaven. (William Shakespeare)

Ignorance, the root and stem of all evil. (Plato)

In the dark pitted furnace of my mind I continued to rise and somewhere the heat ceased as I accepted everything I knew and everything I didn't. Blind, I stood from my seat in the salon and shouted through the sizzling heat and gelatinous egg running as a mask down my face, "Here is true immorality: ignorance and stupidity; the devil is nothing but this. His name is Legion! Gustave Flaubert!"

Cold assaulted me and suddenly I could breathe. I blinked. I was comfortable.

"Wake up sleepy head."

I blinked again and the window came into view. My back ached from the position in the iron lawn chair outside Pantheons.

I smacked once and felt the drool on the side of my mouth and wiped it with a napkin as I sat up.

"You slept for an hour, you missed a lot."

I turned to Twill still sitting comfortably staring into the window, but I didn't speak.

"Groggy? It'll pass. While you return to consciousness, might I entertain you with a parable?"

I laughed. I couldn't help it and through the laughter tears began to tumble. All I could do was nod my head yes.

Twill was stoic, but there was something in his eyes that told me he understood where I was, and he was proud.

"People come to gawk through the bars at the savage, now tame and controlled." Twill took a breath and settled into the telling. "Their fear is held at bay with the beast in its "natural habitat" of concrete and fauna. When he caught his first, he remembered all the rules: clip its wings, bind its legs, hobble it, if you can, that is if you have a pen to keep it in. He was young and curious because… they weren't like him. In his notebook he began.

"I have clipped wings and studied the bits of it beneath a microscope looking like paper crystal veins. I've plucked eyes so that my sight can mimic theirs, for they don't see like us. I have tested chemicals and fire. I have recorded pain. I have severed tails and parts indiscriminately and noted the differences. One day, I thought I recognized a word choked from the screams they often made behind a muffled gag. I removed the gag and for the first time looked into its eyes, rather than through them.

"There was comprehension I thought. I believed I could see and the wretched beast opened its mouth to speak and…

"It was nothing but garbled gibberish among grunts and squeals. Disappointed, I shook my head. They are not like us.

"I replaced the gag, abandoned my scientific hope as fantasy and once again the screams began and I continued to study the effects of these creatures, not like us.

"I removed digits and limbs in the hope of understanding. I continued to test fire and chemicals and logged my findings until I realized something…

"Spread out before me was a body. One leg had been removed, an arm, a digit from the remaining claw, both eyes and its hide which I have found many uses for after hanging outside to tan, but now I realized something...

"On the table beside this one was another, I believe it was a female if memory serves and it too had been skinned. And on each table another, all with notebooks with documented findings and their reactions. Some of these things are different and certainly not like us, but many, nearly all of these here beasts are...

"Quickly I returned to the cages where I kept the beasts with their putrid foulness. They cower as I enter believing I have come to choose another, but I stare at these creatures not like us. They are more than just manner and demeanor as per my hypothesis."

"Just then there is a knock on the door and my assistant entered for the day. I looked into his eyes for a moment, never through, but into. Scalpel in hand I raised it and before I knew it I began with a fresh notebook and a clean table. With him, I began.

"He *was* one like me and now, *he* is one like them. Beneath this tissued mask the questions have been answered.

"I have made quite an unpopular discovery. Beneath the organ wrap they *are*, like us. Indeed we are identical.

"Into the cage I step once again and they cower then scream as I select another. It fights around the lariat as I drag it out, kicking and snapping as the others did. But rather than a table I sit it on a chair. I remove its gag and the lariat. I look *into* its eyes, rather than through and forcefully, I point to my chest and speak a word, a single word over and again until I believe it understands.

"Then I wait and wait, and slowly its fear abates just as mine had. And like us it points to its chest, and then it tells me its name."

Pangea

I BLINKED and took a sip from my cup that had somehow been refilled and in the several hours of time spent here I had forgotten what was in it. I tipped the cup and let it fall into my mouth. It was water, at least I thought it was water, but as it moved down my tongue it began to taste different. A light flavored sweetness came after it and as I swallowed, it filled me as I would imagine an elixir. It was exactly what I needed. I drank thirstily until I was certain I had enough, not too much, and I realized then it had been much more than one cup could have supported.

Across the table Twill was looking at me smiling.

"What?"

He shrugged and turned back to the window.

There was still liquid in the cup and I popped the top and peered inside. It was sill almost full of water.

"Yes." Twill said.

"What?"

"Water."

I put the lid back on the cup a bit bewildered but now just accepting. "I have a question for you?"

Twill nodded openly.

"That story sounded true, rather than a parable like the Pegasus story."

Twill nodded.

"Well?"

"Well what?"

I stared at Twill frustrated.

"You said you were going to ask a question."

"Is it based on truth?"

Twill stared at me a moment and I knew the response before he asked it. "What do you think?"

I stared at him, staring at me. I wasn't frustrated. I didn't feel tired or angry or held to any level of assumption. I was alive. "I believe there is truth in all things, perceived or not. All things spoken are based on some level of reality whether accepted or not, all things have something of truth to them."

Twill smiled and as he turned back to the window I thought I saw his beard protruding just a little as if his jaw was showing that air of pride. "Very well then."

I turned back to the window. How long have I really been here? I thought and just as quickly the thought was followed by, 'does it matter?' followed by 'no'.

Something was wrong. I stared through the glass trying to see what was out of place. It was almost like a different coffee shop. The girl in the red shoes had packed up and was sitting on the side with her friends, still talking and laughing with here large teeth that were just perfect. In fact everything was perfect. Twill said I had been asleep for an hour. Okay, I remembered this part of the night, the couple had gone, the girls had gone, though in the several times I had run through this scenario I never had the girls sit with us, not until Twill brought them over. The couple I was speaking to was…oh yes now sitting at Rasha's table. The crowd was still lively. It must be around ten thirty or so.

Something was still wrong though. The manager was behind the counter and there was the front table, but… I scanned the coffee shop. The English guy was gone! "Where…?" I looked again and again, checking each face, the tables outside, up the street and down, there was Drover. He looked asleep. "Where is the guy at the front table?"

"Excuse me?" Twill asked as if he didn't know what I was thinking already.

I made a face. "You know who I'm talking about."

Twill looked at me with a curious gaze.

"The English guy that sits at the front table, reading and drinking tea, where is he?"

"I am afraid I don't know what you are talking about." His tone was deeply condescending.

I wasn't in the mood to argue or fight so I just sat back again. The entire place was different, felt different. I looked up the street at Drover asleep and…? "What the fuck?" I stood out of my seat and looked around. The entire street had changed. "Where…? How…?" Wherever I found myself right now had absolutely no bearing as to where I began.

I know this coffee shop. It is exactly five blocks from the bookstore… which is where I left my car… after? After following that big sonofabitch here! Where the fuck had he gone? No, that wasn't important now, what was important was where the hell was I?

Everything seemed normal, but Pantheons was now located in a downtown area. A winding island separated both sides of the street with trees decorated in white lights for as far as I could see one way. The other went one more block before it came to an end and darkness swallowed the road breaking it with signal lights. Twill was unmoved. The street was mostly deserted except for a few cars, which looked almost new, but all of them thirty to forty years old. I wanted to speak or ask a question, but my voice failed me and in a dazed I started to walk.

"Not to far now." Twill muttered.

"Huh?"

"I don't think you want to wander off, you never know.

"What?"

"The light." Twill said.

"The light?"

Twill nodded and turned back to the window.

The Zone

I STARTED TO MOVE off in Drover's direction towards the end of the street. Drover was still leaned back against the window of the salon sleeping half inside the pot. The lights were off and there was a sudden sense of foreboding as I glanced in the window and saw a figure sitting in the shadows of the seat near the far end. I stopped and stared past Drover through the window into the darkness and allowed my eyes to adjust. The chair slowly came into focus, but there was no one. I leaned back, shaking it off and continued to the corner just past the salon. I had almost reached the end of the building when I felt... no, sensed was more like it, because it gripped me deeper than that and I stopped moving.

The air before me drifted becoming stale and cold as if an old freezer had just opened somewhere and everything inside was long dried and burned. The image came before the thought, but I imagined it as something's breath, the absence of any sort of living sentience and beneath that stale coldness was only death or the want for death. A walking carrion.

From where I stood I could not see around the edge of the building, which had been the alley that was my passage here and had now become a street. Sixth Street according to the sign, and Pantheons was now located on Main. I looked around into the stink that remained just out of reach. Wanting to step further into it until I looked down and noticed that the light from Pantheons had a definite end to it and that shard was about one foot in front of me. If I were to peer around the corner of the building, I would have to leave the light to do it.

What was it Twill had said? Something about the light?

Always the belligerent self-thinker I moved up to the edge and the cold reached into me with its long dead odor. Everything beyond was submerged in the dark veil of night and the corner of the building beckoned me, just two feet away and I would be able to peer around the edge. Something in me was holding my chest fast. I knew that something was around the edge of the building that I both wanted and dreaded it into my sight.

Slowly I raised my hand up to my chest. I inhaled the cold and lifeless air of this place and slower, I reached out, watching the dark swallow my arm to its elbow. I turned back to Twill, as a child responding to a parents warning of 'hot'. Twill was watching me and began to turn his head slightly from side to side as the parent silently warns the child once again and I felt a brush past my fingers.

I snatched my hand back in sudden shock as I looked and saw an arm reaching from around the corner. It was thin and long, just as toneless and dull as the pasty dark it reached from and then quickly snatched itself back around the corner. I stepped back, all the hair on me prickling at once in response as a sound I could not identify seeped from around the corner calling to mind images of things to be done with my flesh once I had joined the lifeless. "Whoa shit!" I backed away from the darkness as two sets of fingers too large and high up on the building grabbed the edge. I backed quickly to the table, but now refused to sit, not wanting my back to face the street's darkness around me.

"I did warn you."

"Yeah whatever, where the hell is this?" I was shaky.

"This? This is here."

"Does it have name?"

"Everything has a name."

Twill had obviously moved from questions to exact words, "What is the name of this place?"

"This place, is Alphter."

"Alphter?"

Twill nodded and turned back to the coffee shop.

"And?"

Twill looked back at me with his eyebrow raised.

"How did we get here?"

"We have always been here." His tone was dry and condescending.

My head hurt and I didn't want to think at the moment. I entered the coffee shop and sat at the Englishman's table. At least inside I knew where I stood. The customers seemed oblivious, even the ones on the street. Was I the only one that knew something was wrong? No one came or went during this time as I watched the clock on the wall click it's last minutes to ten thirty as the front door opened to a couple walking in.

I hadn't spoken in the last few minutes, but were I, the sight before me would have readily drawn me back into silence. The man and woman were to some severe degree famous. Legendary! And actually by all rights dead, long dead, so dead that I myself didn't breathe for quite a little while until my body suddenly reminded me and I inhaled deeply.

Logic began to seep into the physical me. 'Look-alikes' I thought though I already did not believe that in the second that I thought it and before I know what I was doing I stood and approached them from behind. I was just about to tap the man on his shoulder when I was grabbed. Snatched actually. I felt myself rise as I was spun, fast in the air and out the door and dropped back into my seat before I could respond.

Vaguely I perceived Twill stepping away from me and reclaiming his own seat. "No, no, no." He said. "Now we mustn't disturb the locals. Don't do that again, it could end in quite an unfortunate conundrum."

"What could?"

"Your haphazard interaction could have you taking up residence."

"Is that…?" I motioned to the couple inside. "What is this place, really?"

"Yes."

"What?"

"Yes it is. Really."

"Who are they?" I motioned to couple waiting at he counter.

Twill smiled a little, "Who do you think they are?"

I didn't want to answer for fear of sounding like an absolute idiot, but if my eyes were not deceiving me, which in and of itself was quite the possibility by the way this night has gone, standing at the counter were Humphrey Bogart and Marilyn Monroe.

I was not as green as I started out at this point and I didn't have to look at Twill to know that he had heard my thoughts and was smiling.

Inside all the patrons acted as if nothing unusual was happening then the girl in the red shoes stood and hugged a girl and a guy as they all said their goodbyes and as they did so, Twill's face showed concern for the first time in the entire night. I watched as they made their way to the door just as Bogart and Monroe picked up their drinks and did the same. Both walked up towards the door and they merged. The four of them out of sink, blending they stepped together for a moment while they exited, their ghost like appendages shoving out head and shoulders in a live churning mix of dimensional lives. "Oh…" Twill spoke. "That's it then." He sat back and relaxed.

My gaze moved from Twill to the conjoined couples and back again as they all exited and went in different directions. The friends of the girl in the red shoes walked up the street while Bogart and Monroe moved quickly to towards the corner where I had ventured. Neither acted as if they perceived anything wrong.

Parked in front of the salon was a baby blue Studebaker, looking as if it just rolled off the showroom floor. Bogart opened the passengers side and she slipped in with such grace I will say I had to restrain myself from running up to her, but they were in the dark now. Bogart handed her his coffee and closed her door. Then he stepped back and pulled a small snub-nosed revolver from the small of his back and stepped off the curb. He moved fast around the side of the car watching the street as he did so and slipped into the driver's seat.

In the darkness shapes were moving on the street and I turned back to the couple who had just now stepped out of the light of Pantheons and were realizing something was wrong. They stopped, turned and looked up the street and down again talking to each other. The first movement I noticed was in the street. The second and I must say much, much bigger reared itself from the side of the building were they were standing. It was too dark to see the end results of what happened when the darkness reached down from the building. It was fast and swallowed the man's torso drawing him up in relative silence as the woman screamed, but her screams came to me muffled and I knew it was because of the darkness. She clutched the wall crying out to him and from the street they came two, three, maybe five and they were all on her. Dragged from behind by her feet she dropped to the ground. Their bodies so dark they blocked all images of whatever it was they did, in her muffled screams.

"Shame." Twill said remorsefully.

Curious Georgie Romero

I TURNED BACK TO TWILL, but my eyes were drawn inside to the manager standing behind the counter looking towards the couple. Her head was bowed with her right hand over her heart and a strangely fierce intense gaze burning in her open eyes staring at the ground. The screams went and the manager brought her head up to again look right through me. The gaze turned into a smile and some occurrence struck. The uniforms in the coffee shop were black, all black, all the time. She continued to stare at me, her gaze getting more and more intense by the moment. To say I was mesmerized sounds wrong and corny, but the emotion held me. I was unable to turn away and suddenly became determined to understand this strange woman and after the night I've had so far, I was not going to be intimidated. Her gaze became more and more focused and direct. Her face was fierce and dark as continued to stare back at her swallowing everything that came at me, peeling layers of her as I delved deeper, awaiting the answer to an unasked question.

Our eyes were locked and unblinking, held together in a single moment. Then it happened that something crossed the verge I was drawn forward through the glass once again, towards her as she came at me. We passed each other and I was standing behind the counter watching myself, through the glass sitting outside staring at me. Twill, still seated beside me seemed oblivious that anything had happened. He spoke and my body answered, then he spoke again. A sinister sneer came upon my body's face starting at me and I stepped back as the woman behind the counter.

I looked around the dining room that in my view had changed substantially. Everything was now old, rotted and unusable. All the tables, the chairs and the floor were so decrepit I wondered if something had also happened to the coffee shop itself.

The people were another story. Dead? Yes, absolutely, yet still alive to some greater extent. Several were older, sick. Others had slashes about their face and chest, some which gushed blood, others with holes that also released and endless stream of their life juice to pool on the floor. One woman had her throat slashed, one body looked so mangled as to be unrecognizable as male or female, some were burned to and charred to black bodies of coal. I turned away from dining room to see Noaisha whose skin was now green with rot, holes had eaten themselves and a heavy stink issued from her that caused my stomach to lurch. I turned away and looked back outside. Twill was just as he was, as was I, but the others were just as living dead as ones inside.

Twill and my body were rapped in a conversation I couldn't hear, but the their actions were much more familiar than he or I were. Beyond Twill I could see the street and now illuminated I suddenly sensed death. Everywhere around me in so many places at once I couldn't focus, one after another then several at once. I sensed joy, regret, pain, loss, wonderment, ecstasy, all mixed beneath so much overwhelming death brought upon in so many ways it was apart of me and as the realization came I turned back to the dining room searching for the girl in the red shoes suddenly full of concern.

The shoes were now faded to pink and she was unrecognizable, an ancient woman with wispy white patches of thin hair falling around her. I had to lean over the counter to see the old woman half expecting see her as everyone else, yet she wasn't. Rasha the seer sat looking up at me with a deep profound smile and skin that glowed. Skin no more than thirty years that set off her young face and dark hair accentuating her eyes that were now completely black obsidian and she looked up at me with those great insect-alien orbs. My head began to ache from over exposure and I leaned back shutting my eyes. I couldn't bear to look at any of it longer.

I was aware of all including my body, breasts and dickless crotch as I moved. I was aware of a power within me, so fierce and intense that I could just reach out and snatch…

I felt something outside of myself, but I was not certain what. A pull, a tug, a manipulation of something I could rip and consume if I so wished? I could see them around me held waiting at bay, orbs of luminescence moving over and above my head. And each one had a name.

My heart began to beat faster and I felt I had to leave, my chest hurt and I felt myself ripped from this body so fast and painful I cried out in my head believing I was dying. My head filled with white light and all I was, was pain.

"Calm yourself." The voice was soothing and I was aware of sitting again.

I opened my eyes and before me was Pantheons in all its coffee shop perfection just as I have seen it, shift after shift reliving this night over and again to return, to this chair, beside Twill for reasons that until now had remained a complete wonder, but with the awareness coming into me, I began to see clarity.

"Really?"

Yes. I thought, looking around at the street somehow knowing that we had returned from Alphter, whatever that place was. I no longer needed to look or speak to answer Twill when he read my thoughts.

"And what has your awareness told you?" he asked.

I am not completely certain, everything is still becoming in me. The awareness is most profound in the self, the I that is me.

From the corner of my eye I saw Twill nodding.

I would ask for clarity though I feel you will only answer in riddles and parables again. If the recognition of this night decides to joust me at its end, I wonder of this dramatic passing unless this stage play I have stumbled through is the catalyst. If that be the case, why are we not able to move beyond the inept prison of mortality. Namaste, flesh is an illusion that we by our beliefs create as reality. Our perceptions lend credence to the unimportant and we connect because sight, scent, taste and touch remind us, but that reality should not be the course if by the word 'Namaste' that fact is recognized I submit the preferment of that reality is already upon us. The reality that has been chosen is not, but to dissect this gift from its perfection until it is unrecognized is useless. In the end we will know what we already knew when the mortal coil bound us and fate's thread caused the intersection. Though many of us deny its nurture and allow the us to decease… it shall continue, and so shall it be… and continue… and continue… until we change.

Giant Leaps

"PROFOUND." TWILL SAID. "When the beginning was, there was one and at first there were two before there were many to be fought over and reckoned. There was a thing brought forth in the sentient split, a great beast black as pitch with a head that scratched the sky. These black mares of the night brought the dark dread of pain. And the It had no name and became legend when It was born. Those that sought It never found and those that found were never able to speak if the entity that tore their companions asunder, leaving all terrified of the sleep dividing night from day. In the darkest hills and forests, things grew.

"It was wild and evaded all animals as a wraith unknown though Its presence sensed. Its existence defined Itself in the hearts of men's contest of ages, awaiting the call to unleash Its hell upon another. Untamed. Uncultivated. It prepared to engage. Only the eternals knew for It became and was…. birthed in a mythic field of silhouettes dancing in perditions molten chaos. One by one the armor clad rose to pit themselves against the thing living unknown in the darkness of the spirit.

"All I may say is that It drove tears and madness with a look. It spat acid and reeked of toxic sulfur. Through dark ages of separation and savagery It watched, as man fought for purchase of lands, which he was not beholden and when It spoke the only word It uttered was 'death'.

"Many have sought answers to this. Asking the Buddha how long will it be before I reach enlightenment? They want to know of the deep surrender that causes lifetimes to wink past. The lessons given to and from the earth, the wind and the fiery eyed old man with the acid black tooth.

"Through most, the knowledge of the teachings are twisted as preachers and tongue speakers speak of life evoked in their name. For far too long has the true knowledge of the Nazarene been lost. People do not see that when they cry out in pain or knowledge, any name spoken refers to the one spirit complete and whole. In the unified love of the living, any thought steeped in compassion is at one with the one true message.

"In the quiet pitch of night, the frightened stir and call the names of saviors, elevating the self to higher levels. The joy they speak of life shows the luminescence of dream and the tales foretold of life in the silent breath of sleep. I love hearing of love and marks tattooed on hearts that remain for all time. The deep, the bleeding, the ones withstanding winter to remain clear for the summertime love-tales passed on to the next generations.

"There are those among you with spirits dancing beneath pussy willows, releasing the head as the sun drips on their feet to wash each toe in gold. They laugh at the sun as knowledge arrives as fermented fruit dripping in their mouths. Colors of inspiration come to release the nectar. The dark liquorice of the past is eaten and my tongue becomes the black fear of their soul, leaving them luminescent beings ready to ascend."

People came and went as I sat absorbed in the dialog. I was not apart of the passage of people. I wasn't apart of time, which seemed to be accelerating. Movement became jerky and erratic for a while, then mouths begin to flap as heads twitch from side to side and faster still as hands become blurred with legs and feet floating erratic torsos into the doors and out again. The second hand on the clock was counting minutes as seconds and Twill continued as I watched Pantheons shut its doors, turn off the lights and close down for the evening, releasing its patrons to the world.

"I am curious in this moment." Twill continued his dissertation. "Tell me now of those moments of you, when life becomes a backdrop. When you become embraced by an essence as a chi removes you from all others and all places.

"Tell me when you stood… on a mountain summit… in the middle of a street… sat in your car… at your job… when that something reached something inside you.

"Tell me of the want to scream, shout, or announce yourself in a barbaric roar of childish laughter and shed drips of yourself to the world."

The girl in the red shoes moved as wraith hovering above the red blur of her feet, talking and smiling as she vanished into the night.

"Tell me of the moments when you have been overcome, when the communion was not forced but granted and you see as never before. When second sight becomes third and clarity answers, solutions present themselves and you leave this insignificance to another existence, allowing the self to submerge and bathe in a drowning pool of acceptance."

The street was silent. Dark and silent and Pantheons was dead asleep along with Drover, still crashed out on the flower box next door. I assumed Twill was finished speaking as the deep quiet of night rang in my ears. The calm rhythmic breathing of the earth hummed in the silent low moan of a didgeridoo. I listened to the underlying voice and could distinguish no voice, no traffic, or siren, no thing to impede the night chill of settled silence.

Pantheons had taken away all the chairs and tables when it closed, but they had neglected to pull ours in. I didn't see the gypsy woman Rasha or the manager leave and now I stared at a dark reflection of myself in the glass beside Twill who I was certain awaited my answer to his speech. But I wanted to sink into the mood, giving the night as much of a voice in the conversation as I have when the silence is breeched.

I inhaled.

Released.

Again. Deeper and longer feeling my chest and belly expand fully then slowly I allowed the release.

I began and still I didn't speak but drew the silence to tell my tale with a mental call.

I hear a voice in omen, fortuitous in its unhinged boast. Unhinged as a sad fragment of variegated wondering hopes from the madness I have once seen manifest in the dark magic of night times life. There is in me an inward itch burning me deeper than Dante's stygian pit and it is begging for release.

This thing, apart of me, living, organic and alive, I breathe and that breath is stolen by the wanton fury. I eat though my hunger remains unsatiated by its leach. No other company, by physical or verbal orgasmic release, fills the emptiness of an equation that tells me what will be, when it must be.

The self purged by urination and defecation is a rebirth. Each time waste is abandoned and a tongue is released in an explosion it is a self-actuated pyroclastic surge.

The pressure of this power is terrible and if I could cut this timorous gore from my innards I would, to release the pressure on my head, my heart, my loins because an empty pitted void of nothing must be preferred to a tentacled fist whose screams are mimicked in my waking statements of life.

I see fragmented pieces, grounded as dice with glimpses of my gambling work in progress swimming in the dream soup. Molecules attach, grow larger, merging with plotted characters stepping through story lines and in the awakening an adventure begins.

But none of this is new. I have seen longer than many who tell of it.

"Have you?"

Certainly, though I didn't know what I was seeing when I was seeing and I was not privy to speak of it to anyone. Adults never listen to children and I was I will admit a child with quite grandiose ideas. No one could explain it to me. I was alone for the most part. Or at least I felt alone.

"Were you?"

Not really, I noticed the path as many do though they do not wish to follow it. So many are held to places of temporary gratuity and satiated wishes of the moment.

"And you weren't?"

I was, absolutely and still am to some extent, but something in the back my head reaches for things beyond things. I have come to realize this though it is a difficult practice. And I have realized, there is so much stuff in the moment, it is overwhelming. A singular moment outside of your influence is so filled it can blow a mind not ready to experience it. Silence scares people though. Especially when investments have been made.

"And what is it you invest."

Self. Loss. Pain. All of which brings fear and the acting out against the fearful brings us to things people call evil.

"Evil?"

Yes, people 're-act-out' against the fear and our ignorance or theirs is the base of it. "Evil acts" in the mind of the "evil doer" could be from sickness or could be justified in their mind. The ignorance of that is the base, ours to the condition, 'sickness' or theirs to the justification. However the conundrum is that one cannot exist without the other. Good wouldn't know without evil, what evil is. Understanding things, people, places, races, cultures, will bring us ultimately to a greater understanding of ourselves.

"How?"

The mirror. Our reflection in others, or theirs in ours. Of course many are afraid as that reflection can be terrifying.

Athens

THE MOST BEAUTIFUL THING we can do is in the tolerance and acceptance of others as individuals, not easy of course, but profound.

The most powerful thing we can do as individuals is to question, not some things, but everything and accept that only after we have done so, will we accept.

We need to truly see others, understand and move away from judgment. Not be placated by our emotional rulers, never allowing silence, never allowing questions or thought which removes us from the established norm.

I didn't know where my thoughts were headed or where they were coming from and as Twill faded in the dark silence of the night I wasn't even certain if I was speaking to him any longer, but I had found a voice to call my own, outside of my moleskin and away from my self.

If one is to consider the face value of the consumer philosophy, its logical accepted conclusion is the acquisition of things. This main goal of always trying to get bigger better, more, more and still more until... the next big thing arrives, the Jones' got one, so now your stuff, boring and obsolete must be gifted, donated or sold (usually thrown away) to the lesser's in the economic dream world. The re-cycle, allows them to acquire, not the latest of course, but at least it's the next best thing, "one persons trash" and all that. You clear some space in your home and step up. This obsession keeps people complacent in their obsessive need for the unnecessary. The things that entertain us, hold individuals within a justification of this and nothing else is important in life as they face a wall.

You know I was asleep when the world trade center was struck down and when my alarm clock went off, I awakened to the voice of Rush Limbaugh speaking about something I couldn't quite decipher as I stirred in my semi-conscious dream state. I was annoyed. Annoyed because my alarm clock woke me on my day off and Rush was the last person I wanted to be awakened to. I hit the snooze, making a mental note that Rush was excited about something and that he had said the word "tragedy". That was seven thirty in the morning.

At nine I awoke and turned on the radio to the obvious disaster news. Of course, I was shocked and turned on the television to get as much information as I could. My first thought as I'm sure many turned to world war three, this is it, I could die, you could die and every possible logical and science fictional scenario ran through my head. Spaced within these thoughts was a terrifying movie I recalled from the early eighties entitled "The Man Who Saw Tomorrow," about Nostradamus, narrated by Orson Wells. I released my imagination to people standing in shocked silence in front of television's at the laundry mat, in bars, at the mall, some in tears, jaw dropped in silent prayers wondering what it all means now.

The entire situation was my first true glimpse of the possibilities of what a visionary could do, and the dire consequences of real or feigned ignorance.

Sometimes I ask myself what will we say when the Gods return and ask what we've done with this place? We are all bound to one another by breath, actions, by beliefs, different or similar and that is what separates us from everything else. The knowledge of our differences makes us unique, which makes us responsible. Justice is blind I've heard it told. To me that means it cannot see the confederation of stupidity liberating the world with lies. The underlying want of just-us. History is being rewritten as truth with omitted travesties to create heroes from villains.

They say generation X is the me generation and the now generation, but this comes from previous generations who, just as before, are out of touch with the changing times in the world. They act as if everything just happened one day and take no responsibility for the fact that in an effort to make a better life for their children, the want for them to want less than they themselves did, they to some very real extent perpetuated the degeneration of values, taught or forced on them and resulted in turning them into the "responsible adults" they are today.

The leniency, which began the "spare the rod spoil the child" campaign, started a trend that is now finding its logical conclusion.

I was raised by the 'you don't know shit', 'seen not heard', 'listen to your elders' generation, but I will not blame then for the state of affairs. I will hold them accountable for allowing it to continue. For not telling me change can happen, to not accept the status quo.

Today we are more familiar than the elders, because nothing has been hidden from our eyes and when asked, somewhere someone will answer all questions. Parental words sugarcoated and downplayed do not work because things outside the homestead will gladly explain in as much real or factitious detail as you want. Of course those answers can be jaded and biased in a point of view other than a parents want. How is a parent going to explain something when your older if you already learned it somewhere else?

There is no sociological communication breakdown because environmental and media bombardments never cease. Home schooling has not proven to work. Banning and regulating television has not helped because the world they live in is the same one created by television, therefore avoidance is no solution. What sheltering has shown is that when a person steps into the world they either sink or swim. Most adapt and swim after a small adjustment period of culture shock and then it's keep right up with the Jones'.

In The Telling

THE SILENCE OF THE NIGHT FLOODED THROUGH me and I didn't stop. I didn't know where Twill was, if Drover was asleep, where the Englishman disappeared to, the manager who saw things as I never could imagine, or the old woman. The girl in the red shoes was probably in bed with her boyfriend by now. This moment was me, by everything learned and all things forgotten and remembered, I was everywhere and nowhere at this moment touching forever downloading shamonic messages from the elders, ascended. When the answers become larger than the questions it is time to listen when the universe chooses to speak. The sociological mutilations must end and when they do, some will become the rag in the cocktail burning to set the explosion when the glass shatters.

I am swimming through the ether now, starting to forget eight track tapes, black and white televisions, dot matrix printers, Pong, phone cords and my fear of the Bomb. I will remember to forget cassette tapes, big bulky televisions with snowy screens, a time when there was no Internet and the theories that the government did not lie, the police protected and served everyone, and a priest is the last refuge of confidential hop you can always trust.

I am still immersed in the never-ending adjustments of my self, my place, in this place.

The 'me' generation has grown up in a 'now' world that has bred capitalism into all corners of the earth, fostering the consumer credo, patented, packaged and sold. Everyday products, always accessible via mail and phone, are now downloaded, shopped, sold and shipped a thousand times faster than mail order and the good-old-fashioned American garage sale has become a global web sight for recycling collectibles and junk.

Fashion no longer exists. It has become a slave to its own entity, for there is noting now that is not fashionable for it is also fashionable to be unfashionable, negating all that fashion is. We have created a subculture of fashion and accessories to mirror those we are attempting to acquire. The gods of sheik and sway have been stomped out by implants, bling bling's and spinners, rolled on SUV's that shit black holes into the ecological systems of life.

From the silent dark I heard a deep horse-wrenching cough and looked up to see Drover staring at me.

We are the virtually unenlightened, sheep herded, cattle driven lemmings that wake and work in this systemic jungle built on theology and greed. Our parental government acts as if they are overseeing a daycare center and attempt to keep us placid and serene. Propaganda promises fame and financial independence (if you do things their way.) Anyone that goes against them is shunned, banned or cast aside in the hope that they will expire. If they thrive the campaign will then begin to explain that this product or person is the reason: your life is shit, your children do lot listen, hate you and are into sex and drugs and if they are allowed to continue, things will only get worse. Therefore, this person must be found, this product stopped, this place must be destroyed.

The walls of the daycare are covered in lickable wallpaper. We are told to try everything and everything tastes wonderful if you get enough. Get the most because yours is the best and tastes better than everyone else's.

Face forward, be afraid of your neighbors and don't speak to them. They want what you have and will hurt you for it.

Don't turn around, we have your best interests at heart, we will find you new flavors better than everyone else's.

(How does a lawyer say Fuck You? Trust me.)

The daycare is full and over a third of us are asleep. Ninety percent of the awake are licking the walls on a permanent time-out. Behind us are the teachers, overseers who own and operate, 'the decision makers', semi-elected by us to represent the plebian values we have been "taught" to believe in. We are handed sweets and drugs at snack time to keep us mentally balanced and rationally dense. They tell us it will keep us sane (controlled) and from our socio-blurred point of view, just like everyone else.

…and we are very good students.

Response: Ability

I EXHALED. My breath released as crisp smoke into the night. I looked around. Two chairs, a table, Drover sitting up at the flower box staring, Twill in the opposite chair meditating and me. I turned. It wasn't that we were the only beings on the street, but the only ones in the world. "I have never heard the city so quiet." I whispered in my smoky breath as I turned to Twill.

He smiled in his seat. "Peaceful." He took a breath and released it thick as a furnace. "You know every night, every moment is like this, if you look correctly." He settled again. "Are you done?"

I thought about the question and ran back into myself. Clear, letting the words come from the other place once again.

Any of those who turn from the lickable wall are taken, and none notice the missing, though some hear the message.

The vocal enlightened amount to less than one tenth of one

percent of the sum total and do not have the resources to reach beyond the bombardment of the philistine propaganda perpetuated by the controllers.

The "we" feel we have no voice and therefore we will scream (when we feel there are no repercussions) dominate (the below us) flash (when we can gain attention).

With no way to express our unsigned anger The "we" expresses frustration by writing sociological poetry, we burn it into our hearts, we tag or scratch it on walls with the hope the world will see our unsigned anger.

The "we" expresses individuality through clothes and cars flashing fictional lives, screaming momentary success over corporate name brands who will clutter the annals of history with gains in monetary figures that far outweigh their third world expenditures.

The "we" blasts music on car stereos, with modified mufflers, spinning against amplified motorcycles racing each other to the television to watch reality from afar.

The "we" allows more jails, less schools, listening to the overseers tell us "we" can't afford to educate ourselves though "we" can afford death packs of sons and daughters in a terrorist revenge war.

The "we" exploits the underprivileged and disadvantaged, kept apart through fear (ignorance)

The "we" is kept unorganized, separate individuals, living in a world divided by political pawns, manipulated by special interests that do not have our interests at heart.

Money only makes the world turn because it is the only thing short sight can envision.

The "we" must take responsibility for the nearsighted vision that will cause the Byzantine socioeconomic and environmental systems to eventually crumble. The inevitably is that the previous generation will be blamed for the current and future plight. The sadness of this is blaming Fat Man and Little Boy for showing us what they could do.

The problems that we perpetuate can be slowed if not stopped altogether.

If generation X is the "lost generation," the "we" must remember the goal of youth carries with it an "I'll show you" attitude and the attempt is to achieve greater heights then their parents. Therefore, restrictions get looser, wants and demands are greater, and everything begins younger and still younger. One fortunate end to all this is that as self-awareness grows and some will see the path of the everyman and choose the road not often traveled. Unfortunately it is our children who will bear the burden of our irresponsibility, only by the legacy the "we" chooses to leave them, even if the "we" *chooses* to do nothing…

I sat staring at the empty dead shell of Pantheons and suddenly realized how cold it was.

"And?"

"And what?"

"I sat through a dissertation and there is no conclusion?" Twill still had his eyes closed.

"What do you want?"

Twill shrugged. "Up to you."

I turned to Twill and saw Drover sitting beyond. He placed his hands in prayer and bowed his head in thanks. I did the same. "What's Drovers story?"

Twill shrugged, "What do you think? He's here. Maybe he doesn't have one. Maybe he doesn't need one." Twill opened one eye to look at me, "You need one for him don't you?"

"I just wondered."

"You can see. Why ask me?"

"Yeah, I can see. Sometimes I wish I couldn't see and was just as blind as everyone else. No sighted knowledge."

"Evil."

"Evil? No. Why would you say that?"

"That is your persuasion. No sight, blind, ignorant. Ignorance is evil. Then everyone is evil."

"No, you misunderstood."

"Did I?"

The cold was creeping into my bones and I shivered for the first time. "It is burdensome to carry a responsibility like that. The world isn't evil but people don't see things from other people's points of view. Besides standing in a corner licking the walls we continually head in one direction and most care nothing about the people around us, there different culture, race, age, or gender. I get frustrated as well. It's difficult not to at times, but I think if everyone just took a minute to see another persons point of view I think things could be monumentally different. If everyone looked at three people completely opposite from themselves, three people that they just could not understand… I can't even imagine a world that aware. We usually choose to make fun of them instead." I took a breath and watched the smoke vanishing in wisps.

"That seems like a lot of responsibility for people to take on."

"Yes."

"Your talking about changing the world, that's…"

"Nutty?"

"There's that. You don't even take responsibility. No one does today. For everyone to take responsibility for everyone else… well I suppose you could solve anything." Twill snuggled into his seat.

"No one wants to take responsibility because it carries such a negative connotation. How often do you hear someone wanting you to take responsibility for something positive or rewarding? We are so blind, lost and disconnected as a people. For the most part, no one touches each other, not really. Families, some families have that connection, not many. The only responsibility given in families is who broke that, and who wants to fess up when they're in trouble?"

"Would you?"

"Never. Not with my father." My head was suddenly flooded with images of my father, most of them angry or negative. "He wasn't a happy man and my family… we never touched." My voice quivered. "At least not until my sister was born. The only touching my brothers and I had were fighting with each other. Outside of that getting "disciplined" by my father. In fact we never said love except in a general sense, but when my sister was coming up… I have to say it was like this interactive pet that got into everything and everything was "MINE!"

"That doesn't sound like love."

"Oh, it was because with her we touched, everyone touched at least her. Carrying, hugging, kissing… she was a girl. My mom was a woman and I think had forgotten much of her playfulness, my sister was all affection and emotion. As brothers we were a bunch of puppies vying for space, position, the front seat and the largest piece of meat." I took another breath. "You know it occurs to me now. I have always sought approval from my father and of course never got it. I have a few friends who are more balanced than I, and I know their fathers as well. My true goal is not for acknowledgement or respect from my father, but never once has my father looked at me like a man. And if not a man or equal, at the very least an adult. It occurs to me now that the people I know who have received that, whose fathers look at them in that way are more content and don't seem too struggle or want-for as much. I wonder of it is the same for women. This would stem into the conclusion that much of society stems from parents. Lack of encouragement (genuine encouragement), real unconditional love and pride… they way God must look at us, if God is love."

I turned to see Twill looking at me. Beaming. There was such emotion poring out of him that I felt uncomfortable for a moment. Then it began to wash over me and it wasn't until he completely clouded from my sight that I realized I was crying. I coughed and wiped the tears away with my napkin feeling the inner machismo of my ego seize me, but looking at Twill again I saw that he too was crying, silently shedding great streams of crocodiles unabashed and open.

"I think you may have gotten on something there." He choked out the words, still crying and staring at me. I felt the pride, the joy, the love from him and noticed that beyond, Drover was still staring at me and again nodded.

The silent street and frozen cold of the night bade me to shed and when it came I released. I began to sob again and I didn't hold myself back from the purge. I felt like a child, but quickly realized that it was okay and that this was something I needed and had been missing from my life for what seemed an eternity.

One

I RECOVERED AFTER A FEW MINUTES, cleansed in a way I haven't felt in memory. Twill turned back to Pantheons never bothering to wipe the tears. I wiped and settled again, locked in the moment.

"You mentioned, 'one' a while ago." Twills voice was a little shaky. "I'm curious, who was she?"

I smiled. I always smiled when she came into my head. "Her name was Lisa, or Theresa, or Laura, I never knew for sure. It's feels strange to say we never actually met. She worked at a library. Books were a great passion of mine and have been for most of my life. I was just out of high school going to a junior college and with virtually no money I began to read as much as possible. I didn't have many friends and the library was a veritable feast of free entertainment.

"I saw her one day while at the library and they never wore badges so I never got her name. I learned overtime just by my stalking observations what she drove and that she had a boyfriend who worked there as well. There was another who worked with her that looked so much like her I got confused one day when she came into my work. At the time I was working for a large chain furniture store based out of Sweden and one day I saw her come down the path. I spoke to her about the girl and I she told me the girls name, but I could never remember it, always being bad with names myself.

"Then it happened that one day she came through the store. You know there's a place in New York that they say if you wait long enough the whole city walks bye. I wonder if you set up a camera in each of those stores, eventually everyone within a hundred mile radius would eventually come shopping. Unfortunately she was with someone at the time, a guy, and I didn't have the courage to even make eye contact with her.

"A friend of mine once told me about the universe giving dualities, rhetorical triads and how things happen in groups with history repeating itself and all that. Society talks about it a bit. You always hear third times a charm and things of that nature. So the second time she came through she was alone and I wanted to say something, but I a have never been blessed with much confidence in that department and I didn't say anything again, instead I told my coworker all about her. 'Shit man! Why don't you go say something?'

"Fuck it, yeah! I thought to myself as I went after her. The confidence lasted for about thirty seconds, but I found her and asked if she would like to hang out and maybe do something. She smiled remembering me from the library and that smile was the killer. She had a smile that could stop time. It was real, full and genuine like the ones in Disney cartoons. I would see her speaking to someone at the library she would smile, and I was never able to approach unless I had a book to check out. Once I finished asking if she wanted to have a drink or do something sometime, her face turned to a look of sad disappointment. "I'm sorry," she said. "But I have a boyfriend." I told her I thought so and was just about to walk away when she said. "But if you have any fines…I could…" She was trying to find something positive to say, I thanked her and left. And still I never got her name.

"I must have told everyone I knew about her. My hairdresser at the time, who would later become my girlfriend, actually went to the library to see who the hell this girl was and perhaps find out her name. I always found that amusing and sad in my heart. I don't know if she saw the one or the other that looked like her. Sadly she was placed on a pedestal in my mind and everyone I have ever dated since has always been compared to her.

"Eventually I elected to grow up and I stopped going to the library, once I got a girlfriend of course. I didn't think it was fare to the girlfriend to continue, but I must say, almost every heroin and many many many poems have been written… Not about her, but with her in mind and always with some sort of kiddish hope.

"I saw her one last time. It was literally several years later, but my mind was absolutely blown. I was working at a nationwide orange warehouse hardware store and working the front registers. I saw someone go by my line, just a glimpse of the side of their head then their back was too me. No way, I thought. She was wearing a long dress, plain and light colored and standing in the next line with her back to me. I finished my customer as fast as I could and said "Next person." She turned and oh my God it was her, exactly as I remembered, and not an inkling of remembrance on her face. I was nervous as hell and I thought about what I wanted to say, it came out as, "You dontrememberme do you?" by her response, she must have heard. "You don't want to marry me do you?" or something like that.

"But I'm already married." she said.

"My heart sank I don't mind telling saying and now I figured I didn't have anything to loose. "No. You don't remember me do you?" At which point she looked up and smiled then turned red, embarrassed and laughing.

She said, "Yes," and I finished ringing her up. I had to say something. I figured it was my last chance. "So you're married?"

"She looked disappointed by that and shook her head,

"Forget I said that."

"My training took over at that point and I said okay then have a good day. She seemed more embarrassed at what she said then anything else and got out of there fast and I let her go. I got off register and told a few friends about it and you know I have always regretted it. I figured I should have done something. I should have run after her and said something."

"She's the one?"

"In the context of the one, she is my one, or one of my one's, or the most special one, whatever you want to call it."

Twill nodded. "You think about her?"

"I wonder. I wonder who she was and what could have been."

"What do you think?"

"You know, I was young then and I hadn't really found my writing or my voice. It probably wouldn't have worked out, but then I wonder if I would have found it faster or maybe even taken a different path in life. There are so many answers and possibilities at the same time and all and none of them ever happened."

"What do you mean?"

"I mean this path is what it is now. It never happened and wondering or wandering on it only takes me away from the now of my life as it is. But I believe there are always possibilities and in some alternate reality I did meet and go out and it was perfect. Since there are infinite alternates all things have already happened and will continue once again. All decisions have been made and in each moment we are choosing the paths we find ourselves on."

"You're going into responsibility again."

"You know I do take responsibility for my life, the choices are my own and I can't blame anyone else for what my life is now. I have understood things were my choice for well over a decade. Knowledge is responsibility, and so I take it."

Romeo and Delilah

"WITH THAT REALIZATION I can't blame my parents, my past, my lack, my want for anything that happens in my life and relationships. We seek and find people we have been programmed towards by our lives, our upbringing and such, but if we are aware then we have the ability to change it."

"So?"

"So what?"

"So why don't you change it?"

"Well it isn't the easiest thing in the world. It becomes a part of your nature. The best thing you can do is move with open eyes, stay aware and when it comes time to act, make a clear judgments about it."

"Just like that?"

"Sometimes it's difficult, you're acting against your very basic principles, personal, familial and gender specific. People think relationships are difficult, but it is only because of the preconceptions that enter with the individual. Not only that, but in relationships people change over time. Apart or together, but they do change."

For some reason everything was so open and true in the conversation again that I let my eyes close as we went on as if I were sleeping, or preparing to sleep. You know that feeling when sleep takes you, that singular moment of bliss and you wake from it shocked remembering a two second dream and you look around, wondering where you are and what's going on. It happened. You could say I nodded. My head dropped from its weight and jolted back up startled by the noise and light in my eyes, which fell upon Pantheons of course. I sat up shocked and twisted looking around. It was just as it was earlier in the night. If I were to calculate exactly how many hours I had been here I couldn't tell any longer. I looked over at Twill sitting comfortably as always.

"You know, that's got to stop."

"I agree. I wish you would quit doing it."

"What? But I..." No, I was not going to argue with him. He was right, that much I know by now. Somehow he was right and I had to take responsibility. The girl in the red shoes was back in her routine and singing again. The Englishman was reading. "Why am I doing it?"

Twill smiled and shrugged his shoulders. "Something you're trying to get out of this perhaps, something that has not satisfied you yet? I'm not sure. Of course you should know shouldn't you?"

I stared into the Pantheons looking over the scene again, my gaze falling on the others one by one. Drover was sitting outside staring at people walking by. The manager behind the counter, the Englishman, the old woman Rasha...

"Go on and talk to her." Twill didn't command he simply offered.

I glanced at him then back to Rasha who was simply smiling and staring at me.

I stared hard until I felt myself moving forwards again...

"No!" Twill's voice came sharp and I was back in my chair.

I turned to him.

"No." he said again. "You must go *to* her."

I rose, my legs reacting as if I hadn't moved in a long time. The Inside was alive with conversation moving beneath the song of the girl in the red shoes. Rasha watched me calmly as I stepped through the crowed and up to her table and sat down. She continued to stare at me for a long time and I brought my hands up for her to read.

"No." she said with a slight shake. "No, tell me who she is." She had a slight accent that I couldn't place Hungarian or Spanish or both, I wasn't sure.

"She?"

"The one that started this, the one that stole."

"Stole."

She leaned in close and I realized I could no longer hear the music, but I felt powerless to question it. "You stink of sadness, self doubt and loathing. Tell me why. It was a woman for sure yeah? You're stupid no? Tell me stupid. Tell me who she is, and tell me why."

I felt something seize my chest like heartbreak and I immediately wanted to die. It wasn't an occurrence, but a defense mechanism designed to remove pain especially when it manifested as real. I clutched my chest and felt my left arm go numb, I couldn't breathe. My father told me about this, I was having a heart attack. I closed my eyes and saw my heart fighting my body, beating so fast nothing was moving. My eyes began to water heavily and spill over. It felt as if something was sitting on my chest, perhaps a train or a planet. I choked, my head went light and I was suddenly gone.

"You were not like this as a child."

I opened my eyes to a young woman, the same woman I saw from the managers eyes. "I…" The coffee shop wasn't gone, but everyone else was as if it was closed. Outside was dark and I realized I was, once again back where I was just a moment ago sitting with Twill. Now the lights were on, I was standing in the center of the room, everything was clean and the young Rasha was standing in front of me as tall as my chest waiting for an answer. "No," I was bewildered again but I don't know why, this night had been everything and nothing. I don't see why I should be shocked anymore. I composed myself and looked down at her. "No. You mean hurt like this when I was a child? Untrusting? No I wasn't, but who is?"

She tilted her head to stare up at me. "Not everyone remembers and knows the exact moments of the change, you do."

I felt my chest tighten and my stomach turn. "You know something this is not what I wanted or bargained for. This is beginning to turn into something else and so I think…"

She smiled. "You what?"

I walked to the door and opened it. Outside seemed darker than before and there was no one. The air was still cold. There was no sign of Twill or Drover or the fat man who I still wondered about thought I hadn't seen him since my arrival.

"You what?"

Something in my lower self was coming up forcefully just by her presence, I could feel it. My emotions were rising. I felt like I had to shit, or puke, or cry and I decided to go find my car and call an end to this whole evening. I turned up the street and began to walk.

Rasha was an absolute bundle of energy, the kind of girl you hate of you don't know them real well, loud, very brash and full of life and energy, attractive and very cute. You want to take them out, maybe even have sex all the while knowing they are much more than three handfuls. There is no way to catch a spirit like Rasha unless it allows itself to be caught. The kind of girl that could give and old man a stroke just out of proximity.

She bounced along side me. "Where are we going?"

I didn't answer, she was so cute, I was already falling in love with the attention she was giving me. "I need to go now. It's late."

"Cool." She bounced. "I'll come with."

I did all I could to ignore her and reached the opposite corner and turned in the direction of the bookstore.

"Where are we going?"

Present

I WAS THINKING ABOUT MY CAR and home, but I honestly didn't know where we were headed and the frustration of her with the images that began to rise in me was getting too much. I heard a laugh across the street, the same laugh that was in my head at the moment and my heart stopped. I looked for the source and when the laugh came again I found it. In the courtyard of a house across the street, I could hear people talking and I heard the laugh again. It was late and the streets were deserted and I crossed the street blindly headed for the courtyard. From the other side of a short wooden fence I could just make out the silhouettes from the voices and I entered to five people in a quiet conversation with one breaking into a loud giggle. I knew who the laugh belonged to. There was no mistaking it.

"Is this where were going?" Rasha whispered.

I stared at the group and just as before felt myself drift forward until I was standing beside them. Four of the faces were familiar and my stomach rolled in the darkness. I dropped to my knees wondering why was the hurt so fresh and waited for someone to ask me if I was alright.

"This isn't the same as the other place?"

"What?"

"They can't see you?"

"But how is..." I couldn't even bare to think about what was happening. They were in such a jovial mood and the only common link they had was me so what was happening. I felt Rasha's little arms grab me and help me up. She was amazingly strong.

"Just stand up. What the hell are you afraid of you big baby?"

I looked around. There were five, three girls and two guys. I dreaded the topic and wondered how all of them came together.

"He is who he is." one of the girls said.

"Asshole." another one said.

"He will freely admit that, but there is more."

"I figured I was holding him back or something. I'm glad we ended it because I wouldn't have met," the third girl leaned over and took the hand of the one person I didn't recognize.

People often talk about being a fly on the wall. This shit was not very fun. I was standing on a patio with three ex-girlfriends and one that I guessed was a fiancé and another that was no longer a friend. Each of the wounds was as fresh as the day they had ended. And the love I still carried in me and I watched as if they had all met at my funeral or something. "Am I..."

"No don't be stupid. What would be the point of this if you were?" Rasha said, you're not Scrooge.

"I don't know what the point of this is now."

"Look we are not going to stay long I just wanted you to... besides, this is you doing all this, not me."

"How the hell did they all come together like this?" The hurt moved on so many levels I couldn't focus on anything except it.

"What did you need, want or hope to gain from them?"

I was an island unto myself at the moment and thinking straight was not my specialty, especially when...

"When you are faced with heart matters."

I looked at her, Twill's sarcastic tricks only served to piss me off now will all of this happening I felt truly done and betrayed, even more than the ex-friend that seemed to be staring at me from the group right now. I was Scrooge. I was being fucked with and made into the butt off the laughter and everyone's joke. Including Rasha and Twill. This was enough. I turned and walked out.

"Where are you going?"

I froze. The voice behind me wasn't Rasha, but another very familiar. The conversation had stopped when I turned around and they were all staring at me. "So you can see me."

"Of course we can see you. We called you."

"You?"

"Well a part of us answered you when you asked and we came together."

The young bouncy Rasha was gone and I was alone with the five.

"Think of it as a paradigm shift of some sort."

"What? That isn't the way you talk."

"That is because we are not us, only the parts of us that connect with you and those parts are connected to everything and so..."

"I understand. You know I have had a hell of a night and I don't think I am interested in all of this coming up. The pain and the hurt I associate with you all in this. I don't want to get into it. I don't want…"

"Answers? I believe that's why we came here, well somewhat. This isn't a confrontation. This is a gift as I understand it. It is love."

"Love?"

"We are the manifestations of the love you had and we have for you."

"Have?"

"This should be a lot simpler and easier. Stop thinking for a moment and allow yourself to feel and see."

I made an attempt to release, but after everything I had gone through and done s far, it wasn't happening now.

"You must release, I haven't seen you in ten years and you are still held to some sort of open ended hope or want. Her five years," she pointed to another woman I recognized in silhouette. "Her, two years."

I looked at the third girl and the man standing beside her and felt the hate rise and burn with fevered freshness.

"That is exactly what I mean."

"Where are we going?" The bouncing Rasha appeared at my side again.

"What? Where did you come from?"

"I only come when you loose control." Rasha said. "You're getting angry again."

It felt strange, but I realized that Rasha seemed to drain the anger from me.

"What hurts so much?" One of the girls asked.

"I lost you all."

"And, you found us all as well. And you will find again. And you have I might add…"

Images began to move through their faces and moments out of the temporal context of my mind or imagination. I had lived and loved.

"We all search, some more than others of course, your questions are not of the search, but if the possession in the finding. You give yourself to an image and when that image is neglected you sabotage or sever the connection. You must understand that you too have caused pain."

My mind flashed again this time to hurt and tears brought by me and over me, affecting others in the world not connected to me. "I cannot be responsible for people I don't know."

"Why not? Responsibility, isn't that what you spoke of? Responsibility. Everyone understanding that their actions have an effect albeit positive or negative on others not directly related to them."

I couldn't argue, but I tried. "But I didn't bring your baggage into us."

"No. No you brought your own. And we all dealt the best we could with yours as well as your own. The hurt that you feel is taken from your abandoned loss."

"And the betrayal?" I stared at the couple in the back the girl and the ex friend standing in the darkness, neither of them had spoken.

The girl in front of me turned for a moment and sighed. "Perhaps some thing's could have been handled differently, but we each choose how we react to a given situation. Perpetuating the hate doesn't aid anyone."

I felt my spirit attempting to smooth the emotion, delving into understanding and trying to accept love, but I wanted to hate. Ignorant of myself, the future, and only wanting to possess what I didn't really want.

"It is okay to be angry and hurt. It is okay to own it and express it, but hate seething inside only becomes a cancer, which will consume a soul. No one can fully understand the reasons for some things as a rock is thrown into a pond the ripples effect everything to some degree to their core, visibly or not, positive and negative. To hate the rock is to give energy to a thing which gives and feels nothing for you."

I was numb and hurting from every direction, but my tears had been spent a while ago. I looked over at the one person I didn't recognize and suddenly I did. "Husband."

"No, not yet. Maybe someday and he feels affection for you for what you brought to me before I found him. Your effect on me effected a life your didn't even know about."

"Where are we going?" I looked down beside me at Rasha and the courtyard conversation returned once again as if I wasn't even there.

"I don't know." I said walking out of the courtyard.

"Was that her? Did you get what you wanted?"

"You know I am not certain, but I am okay, or at least I will be. Eventually."

I began to move down the street with Rasha beside me, back towards Pantheons when I suddenly realized that I hadn't walked into the courtyard. I had projected myself there. I looked down at Rasha bouncing as she looked up at me smiling. She turned and I followed her gaze across the street to me. It was me walking down the street and away from us with the bouncing girl beside me. I looked harder and realized it wasn't Rasha. This girl was taller and larger than the bouncing girl's little waif-like frame.

"Hey I'm not that small."

I began to release and move back to myself until I felt a hand in my arm. I looked down at Rasha who suddenly had a very serous look in her face. She shook her head. "It isn't time for you yet. Right now the other selves are getting acquainted. C'mon." She took my arm as I looked back again.

I looked happy. I hope I was.

"And there it is?"

"What?"

"That thing you thought was dead."

I knew what she was talking about and decided not to answer.

Pixy

"So I guess you're here to show me things as well." I wasn't asking a question, merely commenting to myself, but Rasha decided to answer anyway.

"Am I? What am I doing? Showing you? Showing you what?"

"I don't know." The walk back to Pantheons was taking longer than I thought. "She lived in the shadow if her barrio and beneath the loom of her mother long dead in a car accident, less than five miles away. She had no real father and the frustration from a domineering abusive brother had her grown wise in her years. We spent time together talking as she cut my hair before we began having and loving each other inside. Then the idiosyncratic fear bore from both our parts emerged. We grew. We changed and fought and ended it back together more times than memory will ever recall and I think of her now as the wondering about a friend spent intimate more nights than years. My heart speaks of contact, which should have been kept to some degree, but pride is a willful bitch and in those days we were bursting with it."

"Her?" Rasha asked.

"Yes." My voice was hollow and I felt a small lump in my throat.

"What is the story?"

"It's past."

"No."

"No?"

"No. It was only a moment ago."

"The what's and why's no longer matter for any of them, but I will say that whenever I see a dark veiled woman, cutting hair in a window, I think of her. And I miss her."

"So."

"What?"

"You know I would say, 'Men!' but that's just too easy. It's more like people are just too stupid. Pride tore you away from love and I daresay pride has probably torn you away more times than you'd like to admit."

I didn't answer. I couldn't.

"How many?" Rasha started to dig. "How many that you actually felt something for?"

"I would say all, but I also think it was fear. I was afraid of what certain things meant because that connection had marriage written all over it, then possibly children, old age and death, or to be more blunt, my father. And I didn't want to be my father. In fact a few girls expressed how much they didn't want me to become my father. So whenever I saw it happening I..."

"Don't say it! Don't you dare say you did it for them or anything like that!" Rasha was intense and her tone felt personal.

"Well...no. I did it because they saw my father in me and I felt I had to move away from that." My mind wandered again, so much of that tonight and with the pretty thing bouncing beside me, I thought of all the girls, including the absentees from the courtyard. Most of them I felt love to some extent, rarely had I not. "When the frustration creeps in and my heart pumps my eyes blind to the requited death dance of my spirit. The electric shamonic words from the earth wash my soul as landscapes. My spirit begging for release will break its chains and escape though the exhausted aloneness I have felt will have my end planned. Life removed in a spiral falling away and I don't have enough to pursue. I've lost some in that respect as well, but I didn't think it was in either of our best interests to continue in a lie. I never wanted to be in a lie, whether known, unknown, justified or not, when I step out and look back it must be right or it must end."

"You're very inventive." Rasha said. She was bouncing again. "Do you believe all that bullshit, I mean really believe it?"

The night swallowed me. I was the only man in the world walking on the street alone... but, I thought about myself behind me walking with someone. I wasn't even myself right now. I was my other, the observer of everything. Or was I the self and my other the observer? No that couldn't be, because I am the consciousness removed and as life is observed then therefore I am the observer. "I want to believe it."

"You're just scared like everyone else. Just as smart as you are thick! Aren't cha?"

"You know the stupid thing is, I have dreamt of that one for a long time and I don't know if it's real or not and as I ask myself about being ready my answer has always been no. Never far from mind sight, I can smell her with my tongue and hear her voice on my fingertips. The wind blows her heartbeat to mine and I can do nothing but accelerate. The wheezing of my chest's labor has me wishing to become my other self. And speaking to this bewitching wraith. I can remember wishing upon stars in the silent dead of a mountaintop night. She is a mestiza, dancing around me. I have heard names spoken in the glinting reflection of the sun. I have seen her smile in an empty breeze and in the lidless dark I have seen her face in the swaying of trees. This song is played in the sand beneath an ocean breaking against the walls of an hourglass."

"You should write some of that stuff down."

"You think?"

"Yes. You know you would be a good book. I mean I don't really read very much, but if you wrote a book I would read it."

"I looked at her."

"Honestly, I would."

I smiled, "Well I'll let you know."

"At least write it for her."

"What do you mean?"

"You ever read Calvin and Hobbs?"

"Sometimes."

"I love Calvin and Hobbs. You know the world could be such a fun place if everyone read Calvin and Hobbs. They have most intricately simple philosophy about life and besides that they are really funny. I love his snow people." She laughed and skipped again. "Anyway there were a few strips I remember. Once Calvin wrote a letter to himself in the future. The strip was so interesting, full of wonder at how I haven't seen the things that you've seen, done the things that you've done, sort of like a two-day time capsule. I don't think we do enough of that really. Imagine writing a letter to your self a year from now."

"Well it makes sense from the mind of a child. Two days go by in a heart beat as an adult and an adult would probably remember what he wrote."

"True that's why you do it for a year, talk about your plans, your accomplishments, your hopes. Imagine holding yourself accountable for yourself." She sighed. "Your so cynical."

"Am I?"

"Yes. Hey self did you do the things you said you were going to do twelve months ago? How were the holidays and remember that person you were so on about did you go out are you still seeing them or what? Imagine that. You have to allow your self to release more. In fact the worse thing, according to Calvin is that he can't write back. I don't know why it always made me sad to think it would always be a one way conversation, of course for some of us it isn't."

"What? What do you mean by that?"

"You know the secrete to growing old? When you're young, you can hardly see forward into the next day let alone the next month or year. You ever wonder why that is?"

"Yes, but I've..."

"They say that once you hit eighteen time starts moving fast, then at twenty five it gets even faster, then faster still at thirty."

"It feels like that."

"It's because when your young everyday is new, everything is new and you're discovering something new, almost every moment comes to you in a frozen frame of time. As you get older you get more and more locked into routine. Even raising a family. People say they grow up too fast because even then you're locked into a job of everyday doing instead of being, instead of experiencing the time with your children when they are discovering. We all have the same amount of time. The trick is it's how you spend it that makes it special in the context of every moment. You know I'm surprised you don't know that you spoke of it yesterday."

"I did?"

"Yes to those girls out in front when you were speaking about time."

"Oh yeah, time." I thought of Sandra and Evelyn. "Wait yesterday? What the hell does that mean?"

Rasha looked like she had let something slip that she shouldn't have. "Tell me something."

"No what did you mean by that?"

She started skipping, "What? Oh because it's tomorrow, you

know it's after midnight."

Her words slipped in me, but something felt strange about it. "Oh, okay. What do you want me to tell you?"

"If you could tell her, whoever she is, something now from the past to the future from who you are now what would it be?"

. . . And Back Again

I STARED AT THE BOUNCING GIRL who was not bouncing now, but staring back at me with a look of serious depth. I exhaled and looked up the street where myself and she were now out of sight and… "I see echoes of you in longing stares from the faces of ex's. I hear your voice reflected in a possibility that stalks unfound beneath the shimmy of street corner profiles. I am the ghost in your reality, haunting. A precognitive vision of your memory lost to heartbeats stolen by sand dripping under glass. I search in my wait as your wraith watching you stroll through a churchyard, dress dragging, veil soiled, feet caked with bare grime waiting to vanish in your mist. I know the burning fusion of alone that speaks of forever. I have felt the torture of tragedy, both Shakespearian and Greek as the gods laugh at our folly. I am telling this now because I am seeing this now. You must understand this does not cheapen my thoughts when I present these, for I loved you long before we knew and dreamt us as our spirits danced across the sandman's sea. We have not encountered our crossing, but when, if I or my voice is lost to the breath of time, your other will know me as this one sees."

I turned back to Rasha who had such a pained look on her face. Then she turned suddenly and walked away.

"What?" I called. She didn't bounce. She was walking, so fast I was having trouble keeping up with her. "Isn't that what you wanted?"

"Yes that's what I wanted, so many want that, you know."

She slowed her pace and I caught up to her walking, staring at the ground and I stayed beside her until she suddenly stopped.

"You know how many lifetimes you can go before you find that?" Rasha was sensitive and it showed in her tone.

"No…I…"

"A lot." She looked up at me, "or none."

"You mean it's rare."

"No I mean it is common, but… so few recognize it. Or should I say, so few allow themselves to recognize it. Some of the things I have heard you say go so deep into these things. All of the pent-up angst people hold in, trying to create a person into a profile and they into you until you are both either lost or unrecognizable to each other. Many, many, many lifetimes of searching for the one that fits, lock and key, Romeo and Juliet, kismet, providence, no change necessary. However, daily are ones' met and found that could be and though the other selves know the release of the conscious ego self to allow the connection with the others is rare. If the connection is made the reality must come in and allow completion. I find people are mostly unwilling… afraid."

"Ignorant."

"Ignorant. Yes, but to answer your question again, I must ask you, how many have you had and dare I say…"

"Chased away?" Rasha nodded and I turned away, taking my turn to look down. "There were a few that loved me, saw the potential and were wanting and willing."

"Why would a person deny themselves happiness?"

"Fear…ignorance, like I said I don't want to become the dysfunction I came from, but I don't know how to be something other than what is inherently in me to become."

She turned me around holding my shoulders and looking right into my eyes. "We all have the power to choose who we are and who we want to become and that is not a grand scheme as much as it is every moment of everyday." She smiled at me not as the bouncing girl, but as Rasha with such depth and sincerity I felt my eyes water. "You will get it." She said and gave me the most caring and gentle of kisses on my cheek as I felt myself shift and I caught up with something or something caught up with me. She stepped back as the bouncing girl again, "Ready?" she said jumping up excited.

"For what?" Pantheon's was right across the street. "How did we…?

"What?" The street was still deserted, the lights of Pantheons glowing on the dark street calling me to return. "We have to?"

"You don't want to?"

"I…" I didn't know what I felt. I didn't want to return back to my life, back to the reality, the struggle, the pain of loss, even the highs, the joys of friendship, accomplishment, the great moments savored, the adventures of up and down. Happy would never seem so happy without the sad, of course there is visa versa, but in the joy of achievement when you have worked so hard to make something happen and then you succeed… I was on the other side now moving in and out, observing, a watcher. I don't know how, but I always knew it was here and now that I have crossed…

"It is time to go back."

I looked down at her.

"It isn't fear and you know it's here so you can and will return, but right now you must go back. You can't stay here. It isn't your place. It may become that one day, but right now…" She slipped her arm through mine and guided me back across the street and we entered Pantheons, and I seated before Rasha with her great tender wrinkled orbs looking at me and smiling.

"Thank you." I said standing.

Rasha nodded as I stood and walked out. I took my seat in the lawn chair drained and quiet.

"So how was it?" Twill was perky for some reason.

"Illuminating, cleansing…awakening."

Twill nodded. "Rasha, she is something."

I sat quietly wondering on everything that had happened to me just now, and moving on into the night. The girl in the red shoes was playing as she was before and as I listened through the glass as some people came out laughing. Why is why. One of them sang a bad imitation of the girl. I glanced up at the manager who began staring intently at the girl.

I jumped up fast. "You know she's a friend of mine."

The friends stopped laughing and the girl stopped sing.

"She wrote that song for her brother that just broke up with his girlfriend. I'm not judging, but if you don't like it, at least have respect for someone who has the guts to get in front of people and try."

The girl was about to reply and looked around at the other tables and her friends who were moving away from her. "Sorry." she said and went to join her friends.

I looked at the manager, she was back to her business as if nothing happened. The smoking kid gave me a nod and when I took my seat the couple did as well. I looked in the window to the girl in the red shoes. She caught my eye and gave me a quick nod of thanks. I smiled back at her.

"Why…did you do that?" Twill asked.

"I don't know. Someone should say something. We all need to take responsibility for the world you know. It's so funny that there are codes and ethics to doing the right thing. If people are making fun of someone of another race, gender or sexual persuasion, someone from the same situation can't come to their aid. It takes a person from the insulters group to stand up for the other person."

"Why is that?"

"I don't really know. Wrong is wrong. Everyone should know it and not need to be told. It must have been simpler back in the day."

"When?"

"I don't know, ancient times before industry."

"You mean when slavery was rampant. You can't even fathom how many tribes and races were extinguished for the very reason you're talking about. Some of the ancients were enlightened, but not all of them."

"The Aztecs the Mayans."

"Oh no, those are just the ones that were large, popular by discovery. There were others that were just as and even more advanced in some cases. Some that you will never discover, but since you mentioned them I will tell you a secret. The Aztecs knew of the other side and of the return. They knew that death was not but transition and not evil, or painful, or bad, it was honor and they knew it so well that the game they played you have taken football and soccer from, those players played themselves to death. They played to their end and when it was finished, the winners were beheaded. The steps of their temples ran red with blood on the solstice. There were tears of joy and happiness at these ascensions and at the anticipation of their glorious return each morning and in the cry of each new birth. There was belief and faith unquestioned. Today many look for the secure conformity bannered under a shroud of all things bad, shunning free expression and whenever they see others climbing the temple of knowledge they want to break it down.

"What people don't seem to understand is silence is not

golden. From the mouths of babes they say. Rasha spoke of some things that were juvenile. Children must be heard because in the end, that is the voice that is going to speak through you and your future is only graded on how you raise them and by the tools you give them to work with. Expression is necessary for all. It is a release. It is driven plooms of volcanic passion big or small and must erupt. Often organic, sexually orgasmic directly from your own truth, connected to the other side.

"The artists know this. Art is drawn, colored, splattered, photographed, molded, cut, until the creator says done. You are all clay to be molded and manipulated by any means you see necessary, poked, split, shaped my the whims of the creator. Young, wet and pliable hardening over time until you may not give or bend any longer and release the ability to be kneaded. All these choices are yours and you can make them or deny them, but in any case choice happens."

"We are coming to an awareness."

"Yes, but enlightenment for the species could be eons away."

"But that is by choice."

"Exactly."

Titans

I LOOKED FROM FACE TO FACE in Pantheons remembering interactions with each, setting the tone of the evening, this evening. I didn't know who everyone was or the significance of the things I witnessed, but I would in time.

"Sounds like you're leaving." Twill said responding to my thoughts.

"Does it?"

"Yes it does."

"How so and how would that make any difference to this great sphere twisting on its axis?"

"Well as I said it appears or rather it sounds like that is your plan."

"It may very well be and again I ask my previous question."

"Nothing in the answer, but if I may offer. It may be of concern to me in some respect."

"Why should it matter to you?"

"Firstly because you aren't ready as of yet and second because we have not entered a completion."

"Which is?"

Twill took the opportunity to be obtuse and shrugged his shoulders.

"I must say that gets on my nerves."

"Why?" Twill asked looking at me, his mouth widening in a smile. "You mentioned the great sphere twisting on its axis, do you feel differently about it now?"

"No." I answered too fast and as it slipped out I knew it was false.

Twill didn't respond. He simply waited for me to recover from the hasty response.

"Yes." I looked at the old man looking at me. "Everything matters." I looked at him looking at me searching for approval or acceptance and received none. "All things down to the insignificant have their place. Each has an effect on its surroundings, which in turn affects its surroundings and on and out to cause things to be affected." The old eyes made no notion of even registering what I had said. Why is it I feel I'm being quizzed? Twill's eyes flickered. "Probably because I am." I answered my own silent question aloud.

"All things, living or not, have their own energy…" I continued. "Their own signature, granted through its very creation. They may not be animate, but they most certainly have that which comes from existence. We see and feel this often by inanimate objects. Antiques or family heirlooms, worn, used or just possessed for a number of years feel different. Some say it's the quality of the work or the materials used, though when its touched you can feel it vibrate, hum. This is found more in things worn, used or put out and displayed rather than things stored. The vibration is life… a signature or residue of the owner(s) that have been imbued. It is those things, which have an inherent place. They have become use to and within us. We tap and grant these things with our spirit and as a result we are wrenched when the thing is lost or broken. Animate or not, the more personal the item, the more energy given, absorbed, held, the more love, the more alive…"

Twill didn't respond as usual and turned to look inside Pantheons.

I watched patrons coming and going, apart of them and at the same time, I wasn't… Not any longer. Perhaps I never really was. They enter and leave over and again in conversation, alone, hunting for their place while already living in their next, seeking a connection with what for many is considered a myth in their consciousness. If you look for the enlightened in the darkest portion of the night you will see their glow. They are the lightning bugs of the universe. Only the wise-enlightened will follow. As creators, all decide which way is up and twist down into a new expansion of the great paradigm.

"Do they believe it is myth?" Twill joined in.

"Yes. It is obvious. They allow the mundane to affect and frustrate, living in fear of death, which in turn causes them to miss life. They consider life as the most precious thing, especially children. Ironically it is the children who understand and believe with more faith than us. They see no limit to life and that death doesn't exist. Of course people call that innocence or ignorance, but those who have forgotten the simplicity of life hold the true ignorance. They have misplaced the faith of the never-ending and that life cannot end and never will. People fight over the occupation of a borrowed position of the earth. It won't last. It can't. Each generation moves closer to the truth."

"What sort of truth."

"Revolution."

"Oh no." Twill sounded frustrated, upset and hurt for the first time. I turned from the window to him staring at me. "That is as far as you've gotten in all of this? Take back the planet, rise up?" He exhaled frustrated. It was the first real emotion I saw rise out of him.

Currents

"May I?" I asked wanting to be sure he was open to hear me out.

"Certainly."

"The true warrior fights with the heart of a lion and the spirit of God for its truth. Truth beginning with thought, turning ideas, spurning a fire that burns, gathers followers into a cult of personality, which begets more thoughts, and ideas become beliefs. The cult is the beginning. It starts youthful in innocence and is often born of fads and current affairs and it ignites fires, which burn out of control. The artists' sing. The artists' scream. The artists' tell ideas which rub ideals the wrong way. The friction is caught and burns. The poets as warriors tell fortunes of the future while fanning the flames to make it burn wild. The young cult will grow in its call fueled by warrior poets raising fists to the Gods screaming be one with all.

"If the world slowly went crazy, how would you know? In a blind world the one eyed man is king, but in the world of the insane the sane man is the crazy one. One salmon going against the flow, it only takes one to change the status quo and that is the first one struck when they start casting stones. In this world of black and white, you must pretend you don't see color and if you do you must make sure its red white and blue. The time will come to stop dancing in shadows and unite when the mature cult rises to become culture.

"The beat of drums will move heartbeats to pump in the silence screaming through daytime routines. We pray to the gods of waste, "Why have we been forsaken?" We spend our days watching, life learning and all of this has heads exploding from truth firing into us like shotguns. Our brains splatter onto cubicled desks and in the foresight we see our own demise, but turn the scope, look inside and learn about the dangers of conformity, unless it is chosen. We are being eaten alive, an oxidized carcass cannibalized, used and thrown away by the spirit, like tampons and carbon copies. These vessels are the biodegradable waste of the universe, ashes to dust blown away. Reconnected to the circle of lives surrounding."

I felt energy grow in me and I had the urge to stand as the words continued to come out of me. I rose out of the chair continuing as I faced Twill then Drover and everyone outside.

"Rise! Pull your self off the rock bottom floor of the pit wallowing in the pity that has you winning and self-riotous, trying to find comfort in your fears. It locks you in a cage when your instinct wants you to run wild on the plains and make choices that change, destinies converge and we recreate bombs dropped to earth through lyrics, verse, rhythm and creation from the first hearts beating in your spirit warriors to fight in this new age with old world philosophy.

Twill faded along with the crowd and I was standing, I thought, back in the base of the pit from before, but this space was not a nothing it had energy. There was a vibration that moved within me out and around to touch everything that felt and heard. And it was growing. In the dark I continued.

"Men will fish for the knowledge and capitalize on the power locked in ninety percent of their brain cavity. Abused, unused and forsaken generations, dumped in the wastelands, turned to dust forgotten and lost. In the rebirth of life the evolution tries to get their fix to feed the Jones of creation. I see the light of the next revolution coming. And it will not be guns. It will not be sticks or stones. And it will not be fought.

"It will be…in the moment. It will be the love for one, for all without care, without fingers pointing. The next revolution will be in the mind of your spirit that core essence that does not feel hate, does not comprehend envy, that simple void that can reach away from you and bring about change.

"The next revolution, will be love."

Noise erupted around me and I came out from my self, opened my eyes to all the people outside standing and clapping. Everyone inside was standing also and I wondered how they heard me. I made eye contact with the girl in the red shoes and we exchanged nods. I expressed my thanks and took my seat as the people did also. Many newcomers had gathered on the street as well and went inside. The girl in the red shoes started a new song and I continued to receive smiles from people.

"Good job." A voice said as they passed and went inside.

I looked up to see the back of an older man enter Pantheons with a woman. They were both familiar for some reason, but they didn't turn as they joined the line and waited to order.

"Is that more of what you had in mind?" I said to Twill not taking my eyes off the couple.

"Yes, that is better." Twill answered.

I continued to stare at the couple.

"Have you figured it out yet?" Twill mumbled.

"What?"

"All of this, any of this. You began very confused."

"This, as in its reality or the reality of it?"

Twill shrugged. "Either."

I didn't answer and instead thought about everything that had transpired and finished with my own conclusion.

Twill nodded. "Very good."

The couple ordered and the man's face seemed familiar. He was much older than I and he carried himself with some elusive presence I couldn't quite decipher. "Who…" I don't know what I was going to ask and why ask Twill?

"Yes?" Twill turned to me.

I shook my head. As the man turned slightly towards me and I… "That can't…"

"You said you understood," Twill sounded as if he was speaking to himself. "And by your understanding, there shouldn't be questions."

"What?" I didn't comprehend what he said.

"Don't question."

"But that..." My eyes were locked on the man.

"Don't question, accept."

"Is me?" The man and the woman stepped outside with their drinks.

The man with my aged face looked at me and again said, "Good job." And they continued down the street past Drover and it was then I noticed the hair and the girl and...I realized that again I didn't see what she looked like.

"Alas. If you just allowed the possibility and acquiesced you might have..."

"I could now, just run up now and..."

"You could yes, but truth be told you don't want to."

I sat back and pouted.

"What would be the fun in knowing? Honestly? If you knew every right and left turn, every person, event...can you even comprehend the boredom?"

"That's what so many strive for Twill."

"True. You speak that as if people understand what they want and they deserve it."

"You know I do understand, but it is difficult to accept. We have taken them from the mountains, from the stars and out of the books. Gods are no longer astral, but local, visual. We imitate and propagate their standing and ours in an effort to mimic. We have created them earth bound. The untouchable. You know the first time I saw an actual celebrity I was shocked to notice that they were just like me. People who put on underwear, eat, sleep and shit just like me."

I heard a noise come out of Twill that was an almost frightening squeal. It shocked me and I looked to see his shoulders quivering.

"Are you laughing?"

Twills head bobbed and he released the sound again. It was so funny and strange I had to laugh as well until we were both reeling at the table. Twill was relatively quiet, but for the squeaky noises which set me off every time. I don't know how long we laughed or even what we were laughing at. My stomach and cheeks were hurting and the tears only added to it. I couldn't breathe and I was alive. It was beautiful and when we finally stopped, again I was cleansed.

Light Rain

"I WANT YOU TOO TELL ME what you feel, what it is like for you to see and know, to understand and not to speak or be understood by anyone." Twill said.

The lump came suddenly to the top of my throat, brought on by something from what must have been years ago. "There once was a little boy." I said almost in a whisper. "There once was a little boy who lived near the woods with his mother. It was a very long time ago before electronics and contraptions. The town they lived in was very small and everyone knew everyone else. In a small hut in the center of town lived the boy's grandfather who was very special. He always told stories secrets and legends of the lost days and times no one remembered. He was also known for something very peculiar.

The boy spent most of his time in the woods where he would play with the ones he considered his real friends, the squirrels, the bears, the coyotes and the owls, but whenever it rained he was not allowed outside. He was allowed to visit his grandfather, which he did, sometimes for days when it was really bad.

The hut was tiny and drafty and whenever the rain would stop his grandfather would do a very peculiar thing he would close his eyes and be silent for a long moment, as if he were waiting for something. Then he would begin to cry, silently in the corner with his eyes closed he would cry. Some said the old man was afraid of the rain. One day when it was raining particularly hard the little boy mustered up the courage and asked his grandfather why it was he cried whenever it rained.

The old man shook at the question and his lip began to quiver, but he recovered quickly and smiled.

"Come here and I will tell you a story." The old man said and the boy scrambled into his grandfathers lap and they sat at the entrance to the hut looking out at the rain as the old man began to speak.

"You know when I was your age, I lived right where you live now, just with my mother. And everyday I would go into the woods to play with the animals and I would have such a wonderful time. It was glorious and I had names for them all. One day while strolling through the forest I came across an old man who was trying to climb up a small hill, but every time he got halfway up he would slip and fall back down again. I watched him twice from the bushes and decided to see if I could help. So I called too the old man and asked if he needed any help. "Yes," the man said to me. "I'm trying to get up to the top of that hill and I can't, could you help me?" I was very strong in those days and I helped the old man to the top of the small hill. When I got there and released the old man he turned to me and said, "Thank you. You are a very strong and good little boy and I would like to give you a reward for helping me."

"I reached my had out to the old man expecting to receive a gift or thing of some sort, but instead the old man bent down before me, looked me right in the eyes and poked me right in my forehead with his finger. I felt my forehead and looked in my hand a little bemused. "There you are." The old man said. "And thank you again." And like that he moved off down the trail to the forest and was gone. I thought he was probably crazy the way they say some old people are, wandering the roads lost and frail. So I forgot about it and went back to playing in the forest.

Weeks later it rained. I didn't like the rain because it meant I couldn't go out to play in the forest with my friends. So I waited inside for three days while it rained. During that time it was very strange because I thought sure I heard the faint sound of music coming from somewhere and every time I heard it I was filled with something so wonderful I couldn't explain it. On the third day the sun cam out and the rain decided to finally stop long enough for me to go outside.

I ran out the door eager to get back to my friends and see the forest, but only got several steps from my door when the most beautiful thing caught my eye. On the horizon from one end to the other was something I had never seen before. It was a great thick line of colors stretching across the entire sky from ground to ground at both ends. It was the most beautiful thing I had ever seen.

"A rainbow?" The little boy said smiling.

"Oh yes." The old man said smiling and pulling him close. "Yes, but I had never seen one before and this was not the rainbow you see today. This was real, solid enough to touch and coming from it was the most glorious music, more beautiful than any music you have ever heard.

I was so excited I screamed to my mother to come and see, come and see. My mother came running out of the hut in a panic wondering what was going on. I pointed to the sky telling her. "Look, look at that. What is it? Do you hear that music, isn't it beautiful and wonderful, what is it mom what is it?" I was very excited and my excited panicked voice called others out of their huts as well.

My mother looked down at me with such worry and she asked me what was wrong. She looked into the sky again and the others followed her gaze wondering what it was I was looking at. She looked very worried and when the rain started she called for the doctor to have look at me. They checked me wondering of I had gone crazy, I was in bed for days, but I didn't mind for it was still raining and I could hear the music over it and it kept me company. It was so wonderful.

When the doctor said I was fine I went outside straight into the forest and up on a ridge for a better view and on there I watched the thing and listened to the music all day.

The next day the rain had stopped, the sun was out and the clouds were gone and so was the thing I had seen.

I never forgot it and several weeks later I came across the old man in the forest again. "Hello." I said.

"Hello." The old man said back. "Did you like the rainbow?"

"The what?" I asked.

"The rainbow." He said. "Didn't you see it in the sky when it rained?"

"That's what that was?"

"Yes, they're called rainbows and every time it rains there will be another."

"Wow it was beautiful and the music was so fantastic."

"I'm glad you liked it, it was your present for helping me."

"Thank you." Then I thought about it. "But why can't anyone else see it?"

"Because I gave it to you. It was your gift for helping me."

"But everyone should be able to see them." I said also hoping my mother would understand that wasn't crazy.

"I'm sorry the old man said, I gave the gift to you and you alone." And he began to walk away.

"If it's my gift, then I should be able to give it to someone then shouldn't I?"

The old man stopped and turned back to me. "Well he said, if you wish, you may give it to everyone."

"Yes." I said very quickly.

"But." The old man raised a finger of caution. "If you give it to everyone, they will only be able to see it faintly and they will never hear the music. And you will see it the same as them and never hear the music again."

My face dropped remembering the wonderful haunt of enchanting music that drew tears from my eyes. "But…" I began to plead, but the old man said that it was simply the only way it could be done.

Before I could make my mind up the old man told me to go home and think about it and that if I needed him he would be in the forest. Coincidently it rained that very night and the next day I left the house when the rain stopped. I went out and found a nice spot up on the ridge and watched the rainbow all day listening to the must beautiful music that would ever reach my ears. Two days later the rain stopped and it was gone again and when I entered the forest the next day, it looked different. My friends were there, but the enchantment had gone with its mysterious majesty. I hunted all day and found the old man standing in a glade staring up at the sky drinking in the sun. His eyes were shut and he breathed deeply holding his breath for a moment then exhaling.

I hadn't quite reached him when he said, "So what have you decided?" He turned and looked down at me.

"I think I saw my last one yesterday." I said quietly.

"Very well." the old man said and he squatted before me and stared into my face. Then in a flash, grabbed at something on my forehead and stood looking in his hand for a moment. Then he smiled at me and threw the invisible thing into the air and watched it go out of sight. "It's done." He said. And picked up his cane and walked away.

I kept going into forest everyday, but things were different now. The animals were animals, familiar and wonderful, but no longer my friends. Days and days I spent thinking and observing, making up stories for the birds, the squirrels and the ancient trees. Then one day it rained. It puzzles me now why I thought nothing of the rain other than I couldn't go outside and I didn't question the silence when it stopped. Then one afternoon I was startled when my mother came rushing in crying out excited over something, snatching me from the hut and saying that I must come outside now.

I was dragged excited unsure of what I was going to see and outside of the hut the entire village was standing in the middle of the road staring up into the sky.

"Look at that!" my mother exclaimed.

In the sky was a great colored arch covering the horizon. It was the biggest, most beautiful thing anyone had ever seen and everyone stared in wonder. It wasn't quite clear to see where it began and it ended as a cloudy mist. I closed my eyes listened intently to the wind as I said, "Rainbows." loud enough for my mother to hear.

"Is that what they are?" She asked staring into the sky as the name spread through town.

I listened to the wind and talk of rainbows, straining with all I could for the unearthly melody to rise up, but it never came. From my stomach the want came with the loss and I felt the tears begin to run deep and strong until my mother asked me why I was crying.

I never said. And ever since then I have tried to hear the song of the rainbows.

"So that's why you cry grandpa?" The tears were already evident now in the old man's eyes and he nodded.

"But I did learn something the old man he said to his grandson." And just then the rain stopped for a moment and the old man closed his eyes and began searching for the song once again. "Close your eyes." He said.

The little boy closed his eyes and he felt his grandfather's feeble hand move over the top of his head as his finger touched the boy in the forehead something began to come through. Something wonderful that filled the little boy with such wondrous beauty that he began to cry. "Is this it grandfather?"

The old man smiled as he felt the echo from his grandson and he said, "Yes, my son. That's it."

And they sat there in the hut listening as the rain began again and the music faded one last time.

I turned to Twill who was sitting and smiling quietly and it looked as if he was crying. "It's like having the most wonderful secret and not being able to tell anyone." I said whipping my eyes with the napkin.

"That's it." Twill said nodding. "That is it." he opened his eyes and I saw the pride and felt the joy in his stare.

What Engage-meant

"So are you ready." Twill stood from his seat fast and looked down waiting for my response.

"Ready, for what?"

"Were almost done, but not quite."

"Okay," I said rising from my seat.

"You'll want to take all that with you." Twill motioned to my spot on the table.

I picked up my trash the CD and my moleskin. "Where are we going?"

"There that may be gotten too here, powerful and naturally forged by the earth, some of which are known, many of which are not. Many of these are beginnings and the others are ends. We are going too a beginning."

"And I can't know."

Twill smiled. "Ever been to Joshua Tree?" he walked away and turned into the alley.

I moved to follow, but stopped when I felt eyes on me. The manager, Rasha, and the Englishman all watched and put their hands together and bowed their heads. I did the same mumbling "Namaste." The tears were sudden and unexpected.

I moved to follow Twill and Drover suddenly appeared standing before me with the same hands together in a bow. I noticed the back of his hands again as he looked up and we stood holding each other in our eyes. Then he smiled and stepped back releasing me to follow.

"We don't need tears at this point, you are going to need all your fluids." Twill was standing beside a strange contraption.

"What the hell is this?"

"This is a rickshaw."

"And we are?"

"We are going to Joshua Tree."

"In this?"

"Absolutely." Twill climbed in and sat in the seat. "You have to grab those two poles and pull as you run."

"Run?"

"Run, jog, walk, whichever you like."

I looked at the thing, "You know lets just go get my car, it's a couple blocks from her and..."

"Your car was towed from the lot a long time ago, but no matter, you can deal with it later."

"It was? Why?"

"Well is been sitting and... you know, can we get going this is a discussion for later."

I tossed the CD and my moleskin on the seat beside Twill and got in position, wondering why I even question him.

"I don't know." Twill answered. "Maybe you'll figure it out."

I grabbed the poles, pulled and started to move. It was amazingly light.

"You must understand all of this by now. You've graduated, so to speak."

I did understand, but more importantly I accepted my understanding as the truth it was. I jogged on out into the street and into the night, past Pantheons raising some eyebrows as I did so and Twill took my concentration on the road as an opportunity to just speak.

"You know there are people who see the world in the reality of a cartoon, as of anything, through influence or manipulation can be done. They conduct themselves as if everything is simply a realistic illusion of matter, which doesn't. Disney described everything they accomplished as magic with Mickey as the wizard alchemist, but Loony Toons was the true purveyor of this theology. Without explanation characters move through walls, walk upside-down or stand in midair. Those that can achieve these "miracles" are the masters, the gurus, which usually have one thing in common, they all move with a calm air of superfluous peace. They just do, as situations call for it. To walk up a wall, stand in open air, stay on a branch or cliff edge, detached from the earth is second nature and we watch making mental notes as if to say, "of course." Many if not all of these situations are usually to evade some nefarious evildoer wishing to do them in for some reason.

"Most of the characters possessing these powers never loose their temper, having achieved the enlightenment of the Laughing Buddha, agitating other characters just to show them their own stupidity. One character does loose its temper often, but only after the antagonist goes so far as to harm someone outside of the main character. This anger is portrayed with the still calm air of, "that makes me mad" then still with a Zen like straight face proceeds to throw an old school spanking beat-down on the antagonist, much bigger than their stature.

"The other characters are followers of the "power," they want to possess the majesty and the goals are never accomplished although they are able to touch it, if only for a moment in the chase as they step off the cliff or tree ledge to confront the protagonist. They end up standing upside down or in midair for a moment, not realizing exactly what they are doing until they do understand and when the realization suddenly comes upon them, of course, they fall.

"There are characters that challenge the creator's philosophy, even question the creator itself. This usually ends up with the character getting much more than it bargained for as the creator uses them as an example of the true power, recreating them over and again in its own image. Throughout these cartoons one can see examples of God, Jesus, Buddha, Vishnu and all other manners of theology. It is those that have achieved the enlightenment who are able to perform the unbelievable acts, though in cartoons there is no death, nothing is real even though as in the real word, everything is."

I came to the first intersection and kept going, I knew which way to go somehow and I wasn't going to question that either.

"So now you understand. Existence is futile..."

"Because we are all gods."

"Exactly."